MW01611238

THE HOUSE AT SUNSET BEACH

Sunset SEALs Book 5

SHARON HAMILTON

SHARON HAMILTON'S BOOK LIST

SEAL BROTHERHOOD BOOKS

SEAL BROTHERHOOD SERIES
Accidental SEAL Book 1

Fallen SEAL Legacy Book 2

SEAL Under Covers Book 3

SEAL The Deal Book 4

Cruisin' For A SEAL Book 5

SEAL My Destiny Book 6

SEAL of My Heart Book 7

Fredo's Dream Book 8

SEAL My Love Book 9

SEAL Encounter Prequel to Book 1

SEAL Endeavor Prequel to Book 2

Ultimate SEAL Collection Vol. 1 Books 1-4 /2 Prequels

Ultimate SEAL Collection Vol. 2 Books 5-7

BAD BOYS OF SEAL TEAM 3 SERIES
SEAL's Promise Book 1

SEAL My Home Book 2

SEAL's Code Book 3

Big Bad Boys Bundle Books 1-3

BAND OF BACHELORS SERIES
Lucas Book 1

Alex Book 2

Jake Book 3

Jake 2 Book 4

Big Band of Bachelors Bundle

BONE FROG BROTHERHOOD SERIES

New Year's SEAL Dream Book 1

SEALed At The Altar Book 2

SEALed Forever Book 3

SEAL's Rescue Book 4

SEALed Protection Book 5

SUNSET SEALS SERIES

SEALed at Sunset

Second Chance SEAL

Treasure Island SEAL

Escape to Sunset

The House at Sunset Beach

SILVER SEALS SERIES

SEAL Love's Legacy

SLEEPER SEALS SERIES

Bachelor SEAL

BONE FROG BACHELOR SERIES

Bone Frog Bachelor

STAND ALONE BOOKS & SERIES

SEAL's Goal: The Beautiful Game

Nashville SEAL: Jameson

True Blue SEALS Zak

Paradise: In Search of Love
Love Me Tender, Love You Hard

NOVELLAS
SEAL You In My Dreams Magnolias and Moonshine

PARANORMALS

GOLDEN VAMPIRES OF TUSCANY SERIES
Honeymoon Bite Book 1
Mortal Bite Book 2
Christmas Bite Book 3
Midnight Bite Book 4

THE GUARDIANS
Heavenly Lover Book 1
Underworld Lover Book 2
Underworld Queen Book 3
Redemption Book 4

FALL FROM GRACE SERIES
Gideon: Heavenly Fall

NOVELLAS
SEAL Of Time Trident Legacy

All of Sharon's books are available on Audible,
narrated by the talented J.D. Hart.

ABOUT THE BOOK

SEAL Team 3 member Andy Carr is liking his Florida digs – the call of the seabirds and the roaring of the ocean at his back door. Sunset Beach is also the place where he found his soulmate, Aimee, rescuing her from an abusive relationship with another teammate – a sticky situation that nearly lost him his Trident.

But they've embarked on renovating the little house at Sunset she found while they were falling in love, and this house means more to them than just glass, wood and sheetrock.

Andy begins to reconsider his membership in the Trident Club and is called in another direction as Aimee also searches the bars and halfway houses for her long lost brother after her ghost sighting of him.

He vows to protect her until his last day on earth, but Aimee can run into trouble all her own, especially when he's gone overseas.

Now that they've found the perfect love, the perfect house to consider laying down roots and raising a family, will echoes from their past destroy the harmony of their romance? Andy always fights to win, but what if he loses?

AUTHOR'S NOTE

I always dedicate my SEAL Brotherhood books to the brave men and women who defend our shores and keep us safe. Without their sacrifice, and that of their families—because a warrior's fight always includes his or her family—I wouldn't have the freedom and opportunity to make a living writing these stories. They sometimes pay the ultimate price so we can debate, argue, go have coffee with friends, raise our children and see them have children of their own.

One of my favorite tributes to warriors resides on many memorials, including one I saw honoring the fallen of WWII on an island in the Pacific:

> "When you go home
> Tell them of us, and say
> For your tomorrow,
> We gave our today."

These are my stories created out of my own imagination. Anything that is inaccurately portrayed is either my mistake, or done intentionally to disguise something I might have overheard over a beer or in the corner of one of the hangouts along the Coronado Strand.

I support two main charities. Navy SEAL/UDT Museum operates in Ft. Pierce, Florida. Please learn about this wonderful museum, all run by active and former SEALs and their friends and families, and who rely on public support, not that of the U.S. Government.
www.navysealmuseum.org

IF YOU GOT ANY CLOSER, YOU WOULD HAVE TO ENLIST

I also support Wounded Warriors, who tirelessly bring together the warrior as well as the family members who are just learning to deal with their soldier's condition and have nowhere to turn. It is a long path to becoming well, but I've seen first-hand what this organization does for its warriors and the families who love them. Please give what your heart tells you is right. If you cannot give, volunteer at one of the many service centers all over the United States. Get involved. Do something meaningful for someone who gave so much of themselves, to families who have paid the price for your freedom. You'll find a family there unlike any other on the planet.
www.woundedwarriorproject.org

CHAPTER 1

Christmas Week 1980

HANK BORGES SCANNED his living room at the house he'd rented at Sunset Beach on the Florida Gulf Coast. It didn't feel like Christmas. The sun was too bright, the weather too warm. He didn't even have a Christmas tree. It felt like the middle of the summer in New York City.

There were more crumpled pieces of paper lying all around him, making him into a human hamster, than acceptable pages of his manuscript stacked neatly in a box on his right. It might've made him chuckle except for the fact that with this sea of rejected words scattered all over the floor meant he was failing. Failing to get this book out on time.

Christmas didn't have anything to do with it.

Ba Humbug.

As a successful science fiction author of some thirty widely acclaimed bestselling novels, he had a reputation and following much to be envied by the literary world. He was lucky enough to have fans and fans of fans—sons and daughters, grandson of fans—who had read him over his nearly twenty-year career, which was ignited as a struggling psychology major his sophomore year in college.

He'd taken an elective creative writing course and fell in love with his sensual teacher, Miss Cohn, a child Holocaust survivor whose shapely legs and beautiful lips were so oddly mismatched to the numbers tattooed into her forearm. Most of Hank's friends were going to sock hops and dance parties, learning the Twist and the Mashed Potatoes, screaming over Elvis Pressley. Hank's passions lay elsewhere, between the pages of his favorite futuristic fantasy novels.

She couldn't have been more than ten years his senior. He almost stalked her, finding places he could run into her until she agreed to talk to him about his writing—without scaring her, of course. She was a beautiful, fragile creature and Hank's heart was completely enchanted. The rest of the world disappeared when he thought about her.

"Aliens? You wish to write about aliens?" she'd said in her slight German accent. Her honey-brown hair drifted across her face as she lifted it back behind her ear. Her smile set his heart on fire.

Did she know?

"I love reading science fiction," he'd stammered.

He watched her brown eyes widen, was distracted with the crease at the right side of her upper lip. She waited for him to elaborate.

"What is most important I think is if *you* think I have any talent. I have this—" he hesitated to speak the words but did anyhow—"this *passion* for writing now. You've inspired me, Miss Cohn."

She actually blushed, her long dark lashes caressing the top of her cheeks as she looked down demurely. He'd always wondered how something so horrible could happen to such a delicate creature. He wondered how God could be so cruel. And was it wrong that he was attracted to her? Maybe he'd burn in hell for his crime of sitting in front of her presence, the strength of her womanhood and her resiliency infusing him with something more than admiration. It was a genuine major young man's first crush. His father would beat the crap out of him if he ever found out.

She was forbidden fruit. She was not only his teacher, but she was also Jewish, something his Italian Catholic father would never tolerate.

But when had Hank ever done what he was sup- posed to do? He was always skirting the edge of something naughty. He never laid a hand on her that summer. But he loved her nonetheless, as she edited his first fledgling pages and made story suggestions that made him dive into lost weekends with his type-writer. She was a part of every book heroine he wrote after that. They all had brown eyes and big lips. They all had a deep crease at the side of those lips where her flesh mated in a half-smile.

His agent said it was a fluke. But fluke or no, Hank never went back to college. He never found out what became of her and it filled him with regret.

Now there were two motion pictures based on his book series, and three others optioned and in the works. He was contracted for at least two and hopefully three books for his publisher this year, but due to an editorial dust-up late last year, he'd canceled one publishing date, bought out his contract, costing him nearly thirty thousand dollars, and had rescheduled with a new imprint. That set him back a good two books, yet, he was still behind for the new publisher. He told himself he was too good—too experienced—to be dealing with this, but that was the truth.

This is rookie madness. He gave himself a quick im-aginary kick in the seat of the pants and shouted internally, "Get over it!"

But as he stared at the grinning face of his IBM Se-lectric typewriter, he identified what was happening. He had a full-blown case of writer's block. The word made his bowels churn.

Standing up to stretch, he walked to the sliding

glass door, crunching on balls of wadded paper as he did so. This sweet little beach house was the refuge he rented every time he wrote a new book. This house at Sunset Beach, had always been his lucky charm. It was sort of his secret dose of kryptonite. Well, not kryptonite exactly, his secret dose of vitamins. His secret weapon. This little place at Sunset Beach overlooking the tiny waves and the sugary sand had always been inspirational to him. The words always seem to flow, and the stories just kept coming.

But this time it was different. As if he had a defective muffler, the words choked like chunks of carbon caught in a filter, causing pressure and an invisible black cloud. He told himself he was too talented to have writer's block.

But that's exactly where he was. He was blocked, tethered to this royal blue typewriter. The contract he was in danger of blowing off would cost him a lot more than the first one he'd bought back. It was money his soon-to-be ex-wife had already spent on God knows what. He was backing out on that contract with her, too, and at an even greater cost. His demanding wife back in New York City, his children and all his adoring fans were waiting with bated breath for his new release for all sorts of reasons.

Sadly, it was beginning to look like he was going to fail this time, again! And just like the grand schemes in his epic novels, his failure would sweep over his career like an epidemic. He had fears that he would never be able to write a book again. That no one would want to read him. Maybe no one wanted to read him now. Maybe that's why it was so difficult for him to write.

"Christ! What the hell am I doing with my life?"

But not one of the menageries of characters in his head answered him. The sliding glass door fogged up, and then cleared, revealing a beautiful, sunny day at the beach. Life was perfect for everyone else in the world, even the imaginary world, except him.

How he wished he could play in the sand like the people he watched through the window. They didn't seem to have a care in the world. There were children with family members parked under umbrellas and on lawn chairs. There were groups of young men spread out on towels viewing groups of young women also spread out on towels. There was generous sharing of suntan lotion. Everyone had sunglasses. Some had floppy hats, which Hank would have to wear, because he hadn't been outside on the beach one day since he'd arrived a month ago.

Well, maybe it was time for him to venture outside, face the ocean, face the sand, face his would-be fans— as if they knew how famous he was. Maybe it was time to get baked like a lobster, wear Noxzema on his nose, a floppy hat. Or perhaps, like his main character,

Captain Sampson and his alcoholic blue vampire android second-in-command, he should down a half a bottle of scotch, hit the warp speed and boomerang to another galaxy in his drunken stupor. Maybe then, as he ached in his sunburned state, he might be able to write again. It might take something like that for him to be able to perform. It would be like lighting himself on fire.

He shuddered. This was bad. Very bad indeed.

Hank's estranged wife was out shopping for townhouses in very expensive neighborhoods, anticipating a settlement that would put her up in style for the rest of her life. He didn't mind paying child support, as he figured was owed, and he appreciated that his wife agreed to have full custody of the girls, so that he could visit on special holidays. After all, he was Hank Borges, the famous science fiction author. He felt uncomfortable being daddy, and always had.

He loved his girls, but he didn't think he was very good for them, and, according to his wife, he wasn't. It just seemed a lot easier to go along with the program she'd devised, albeit expensive. There were wars you could win and wars you never would win. This one was a war he would never be able to win. He'd take a chance that when the girls became young adults, began to raise families of their own, they would appreciate him more.

Hank shed his pajamas and donned a T-shirt and a pair of swimming trunks, along with a pair of zoris. He put on a red beach hat that he had found at the grocery store one year, flattened and floppy. He'd packed it in his suitcase every year he came to Sunset Beach, and although he never used it, did look well-worn. Just from the packing.

Like my writing career, he thought.

At the doorway, he stepped out as if he had complete snorkel gear, flippers and a mouthpiece stuck in his piehole. He felt ridiculous in this get up, but he proceeded to the beach anyway.

He was headed for a little slice of sugary white sand beach between a group of young men and a little group of pretty twenty-something girls working the sand on their knees. In their bikinis and ponytails, they were obviously college age girls, down for a weekend or a week during the holidays, shedding their family and traditions as well, just like Hank was.

It was a cliche just like so much of what he'd written this morning and tossed away, but the girls wore ice cream colors and all with different coloring. One girl was a brunette, with an equally bronzed light coffee mocha skin and complexion to go with it. One girl was red haired, another was a very light blonde. The young lady furthest away was a mahogany-colored young woman with pale peach skin with a long ponytail that extended all the way down her backside to her waist.

"Ladies," he said as he passed them.

They were constructing a sandcastle, all four of them pouring buckets of sandy water to smooth over surfaces. They had built turrets and windows and a ramp as well as an archway entrance, that would all dissolve in the oncoming surf later on in the evening.

He removed his zoris and walked toward the ocean. The water was lukewarm, not freezing cold as it would have been up north, and not like how he remembered the water in Santa Cruz that disastrous summer when he brought the wife and girls. Maybe it was the close proximity to the three females in his little clan, but Santa Cruz didn't do anything for his psyche. The wind was too cold and so was the water. The smell of cotton candy from the Boardwalk made him want to vomit and remnants of it stuck to his pages, to the fingers, to the keys and the bottoms of his shoes. Using the bathroom was problematic so he frequently had to water the ice plant with his own urine. He decided right then and there that Florida would be the only place in the universe he'd be able to write. And he needed to be alone. Complete peace and quiet. Just he and Captain Sampson and Mega Blue.

Except for this time. For a whole month, he'd been unable to write, to even get more than ten pages typed up that he didn't toss as reading like one of his students.

The first week he was here, he felt this creeping sense of dread overtaking him, like the black plague infecting his fingers and his face and his brain, making him scramble his ideas and unable to put one word in front of the other without making no sense whatsoever. Everything he wrote was awful. It was third grade style. It was what he would tease his other author friends having read someone else's manuscript. Amateurish. Not at all like Hank Borges, the famous science fiction author, would do.

But the ocean didn't see this. The ocean treated him just like any other person who stood up to his white knees in the surf. The sun was right smack in the middle of his forehead, his sunglasses barely able to keep out the glare, the floppy hat not helping. He turned to the side so he wouldn't damage his eyes. Apparently, he would need a different pair. These he'd picked up at the beach store. And it was obvious they were only worth the dollar that he paid for them.

The three girls ran over into the surf splashed water on each other and laughed, getting the sand off their legs, their arms, their shoulders, and trying to see who could put the most water on their friends. Their total lack of common sense was thrilling to him. He liked watching them. They laughed freely throwing their heads back, screaming when the water was tossed in their faces, slipping, sitting in the water, kicking, splashing water with their toes, doing everything that a three-year-old might do, except they were in their early twenties. And they were so attractive, Hank felt like asking them what their secret was—if they swallowed some elixir, if perhaps just because of their youth, they had discovered the source of happiness.

Was it that he was unhappy? Was he unhappy because his wife didn't want to have anything to do with him? His girls seemed more preoccupied with things at school than things daddy would talk to them about, except when he brought them lavish gifts? Was it that he had turned that terrible four-oh plus age and thought perhaps not only his writing career could be over but his desire and need for romance might be gone as well? Maybe his dick was all shriveled up too from lack of use. His few further attempts at dating were shameful and embarrassing. He had a performance issue in the bedroom, something he'd never experienced before.

Just like my writing, he thought.

Hank felt the splash of water on his side and whipped around to object. The young woman in front of him gave him a wide smile, her pink lipstick an attractive distraction against her peachy skin. She had Latin coloring, as if she was Italian or Cuban or South American, perhaps Brazilian. His mind wandered to all kinds of exotic places as he stared at her dripping wet, her wide smile and sparkling deep brown eyes with her long ponytail wet and dripping. Crystalline drops of water hung from her ear lobes. She was breathing heavy. Her ample chest made it impossible for him not to come alive as a man even though he'd kind of pictured himself as an old lady with the floppy hat and the pink skin from his lack of sunshine. She clearly was ten times healthier than he was. Who was he to tell her not to splash him, he thought?

"I'm sorry. That was an accident."

He didn't believe a word she said, but he was charmed by her attitude anyway so decided to play along.

"It's quite all right, miss, I think I deserved it a bit." She angled her head and looked at him scrunching up her eyebrows and the top of her nose. "Why do you say that?"

"Because my dear, I'm working on a book, and it's not happening. I'm frustrated, and you guys looked like you were having so much fun, I decided maybe I'd indulge a little bit in your energies. So here I am, ready to receive the ocean and all your laughter and smiles and playful attitudes. I need something right now. This book is never going to get written unless I do shift something."

"Then you should dunk. You definitely should

dunk," said the young black woman. With her hands on her hips tapping her toe on the wet sand creating a puddle beneath the ball. Her frown was mischievous but serious.

"Dunking's just the best," said the red head.

He was enjoying feeling ganged up on. It was exactly what he deserved. He'd been such a worm, a white fleshy flabby worm sitting in that living room trying to write a ridiculous space drama with a little bit of romance added in. The romance was definitely not happening in the book, but even the plot was eluding him, and he had a structured list taped to the wall showing chapter by chapter what he should write. Problem was, it was like he was required to write in Russian or Spanish or something, because he had no clue how to structure his English sentences so that they made sense even to himself.

The brunette with the brownie-colored eyes stuck out her lower lip and gave him an empathetic look. "It's not really that bad, is it?"

"Oh, it is. It definitely is." He turned to face the ocean as if willing to take it all on. The entire Gulf of Mexico and whatever else through the seas, all the sharks, the fish, the shells, everything, he'd take it all. He deserved an avalanche of saltwater. He deserved to be dragged out to sea and drowned like a dead fish.

"I'm a mess." He chanced a quick glance to his

right to see her looking at him with one eye squinted. "Don't you think?"

"I think you're right. You're one of those men that my mother said never to spend any time with. Not as a teacher, not as a camp counselor, and certainly not as a stranger on the beach. But I'm so sorry you're going through all this. I have no idea what you really mean. And like Estelle said, if you run out of options, I'd just jump in the water and get wet and then go right back up to the house and do whatever it is that you need to do and put one finger in front of the other and put together your work. That's what I would do anyway. And if that doesn't work, well, you could always slit your wrists."

It was shocking that she would even consider saying something like this to him, a complete stranger. What if he was teetering on the edge of suicide? It showed a total lack of understanding of the ways of the world. People were fragile. Especially people in New York were fragile. And when they were running away to the Florida beach, well, they were definitely, looking for a change.

He watched her backside bounce deliciously along with the screams and giggles of the other two friends. They ran down the beach several houses and then up through a beach access ramp and he lost them into the parking lot or the sea of houses beyond. None of them even turned around to wave good-bye.

It had been a delightful encounter. Maybe she was right. He looked at the ocean, sat and watched as the water came up to within a foot of his toes. He got up, scrambling to his feet, and walked into the water up to his knees. He sat down and inhaled squealing to himself as the water covered his lower torso and then splashed up his chest getting the right side of his face wet and soaking his backside. He took one more wave, and then got up, and searched for his zoris, repositioned his hat, and ran toward his back patio. He grabbed a towel overhanging one of the chairs, dusted off, left his zoris outside to dry as well as the towel, opened the sliding glass door, and closed it behind him.

He walked around the table to stare at the blue IBM Selectric typewriter that grinned up at him, the keyboard forming gray teeth. He imagined hearing the machine chuckling at him, taunting him, daring him to just try to get a story out of that beast of a machine. He turned the little toggle switch to on, heard it buzz as the little ball in the center of the machine whirred to life, twisting itself quickly and then settling down. The tick, tick, tick of the machine continued. He sat gently in his wet trunks, dried his hands on his chest and then started to write.

'It was the summer that would change his life

forever. Just one trip to the green waters and yellow beaches of Scion, the mythical healing beach on the fourth planet of the Recovery Galaxy. He knew that all the energy he received from the ocean would help restore his wounds and make the upcoming battle his to own. He was conqueror of the worlds of Scion. But he'd been ousted.

Now was his chance to come back, with revenge, and this time, he'd win the war.'

Hank re-read his words and liked them. He'd found his mark, his place on the stage, and now he felt the words would flow.

Her name was Carmen, and Hank got so that if he didn't see her playing on the beach, the day was somehow less brilliant. The words were flowing from his fingertips, and he often rehearsed some of the chapters in his mind as he walked the beach. But he always looked for Carmen. He was planning to stay at the house on Sunset until the 1st of February, or until he finished the book. The girls were going back to college after New Year's.

The girls bought him a small Christmas tree and decorated it with shells.

As the days went by, Carmen had decided to not go back to school with her other two friends and remained at the house five doors up from his, taking a job at one of the local coffee shops. She'd explained to him that she needed a break from school, that her parents were divorcing, and money was tight, so she wanted to stay away from the family, earn her own, let the beach heal her insides and just give the family thing a rest. He felt sorry for her. But he was secretly glad to have the company. Talking to her was good for his daily word count.

"Going through a divorce is difficult. But in the long run, it's better to be with someone you love than to just stay together for the sake of not saying that you failed at marriage. People don't like to get divorced because it does feel like failure." His advice over coffee one day didn't seem to faze Carmen.

"Well in their case, my brother and I felt they should get divorced a long time ago. But of course, they didn't see that."

"Give them time, your parents are going to need you. It's always wonderful when your kids appreciate you, no matter what kinds of stupid mistakes you've made."

"So, you've been divorced and made mistakes?"

"Does God brush his teeth?"

"Big mistakes or little mistakes?"

"Every kind of mistake there is to make. And then a few more. And I'm just entering the divorce phase of my life. I think it's a rite of passage or something."

"You don't seem like that kind of a man."

"I don't know what kind of man I am. But I'll be very poor if I don't finish this book."

He liked talking to her in the afternoons and a couple of times they talked long into the sunset. He never got tired of watching the orange and purple sky, the way the sun melted into the horizon. Everyone along the beach came out to watch. Some dressed in their colorful bell bottoms and halter tops, others in their cutoffs and still other people walked out in slacks and shirts removing their lace up shoes and socks, not really prepared for the beach. Those were all Miami Vice times. It took all types. But the beach was a leveler, some common ground where everybody performed their little drama, in front of the sun, the sky, the wind, the birds and everybody else. And the truth was, nobody really cared.

As the weeks went by eventually Hank asked Carmen if he could buy her dinner and she turned him down. But she did agree to have lunch with him on one or two occasions, until finally she relented and agreed to let him take her out to a fancy seafood restaurant. Hank told himself it wasn't a date because she was twenty years younger than he was. And he was fairly sure Carmen didn't view him as boyfriend-type material. He just liked the way he felt around her, and he liked the innocent way she looked up at him. She laughed at his jokes even though he'd told them thousands of times before. But unlike his former wife and his two daughters, she found him funny and fascinating and didn't neglect to tell him so often.

There came a time when the talk got slightly more serious, he was able to ask her about her family, and about her growing up. And he was struck with how strong she was, being raised in a relatively poor family out West, her parents had worked around and for a large farming concern and had scraped together enough to send Carmen to college. But it weighed on her heavily, the cost of that college.

It happened one night when he wasn't paying attention. The sunset was especially beautiful and after most of the people had left the beach, he and Carmen were still standing there looking at where the sun had been. The glow had long faded, and the shadows of early evening had covered everything, turning it a light gray, purple color. When the stars started to come out, he watched the angle of her neck and the way her eyes sparkled in the darkness and it seemed so natural to reach over, take her in his arms and kiss her. She didn't fight him, but she was nervous because he felt her shake. She didn't seem to know what to do with her hands, but he did.

One thing led to another and he whispered in her ear that he'd like to take her to his house and would she, please?

She said yes.

That night, they breached the chasm of their two worlds in one of the most beautiful lovemaking sessions he'd ever had. It left him drunk with lust, craving for more. He didn't even realize until later when she told him that he had been her first.

She let her house go and stayed with him until the 1st of February. They had always talked about the fact that Carmen would go back to California and he would return to New York. They talked about how maybe someday they'd come back to Sunset Beach and spend another week or two or a couple of months there together again, and they promised to stay in touch. He said he'd write her letters and took her address. She promised to answer his letters and to buy his new book when it came out.

But as the weeks went by, the book that Hank wrote become a bestseller and he became involved in the promotion, the book tours, the signings and the publicity. He intended to write her, and then he caught himself thinking that perhaps she was better off without him. The age difference didn't matter in the bedroom between them. But he'd had a life and he was going to have to deal with the mistakes of his past. He had girls that were ten years younger than she was. He was a responsible father, businessman, and he belonged where he had grown up in New York City. Carmen had her whole life ahead of her and Hank didn't want to take that life like he'd taken her virginity.

It wasn't until many years later that they met again.

And then, they were inseparable.

CHAPTER 2

Christmas Eve Day 2020
Wedding Day

ANDY CARR WOKE up in the guest bedroom, upstairs, because Aimee had invited several of her
girlfriends to spend the night and he knew what their
chitchat would do to his sleep pattern.

Today was the wedding day. The date had been
postponed twice, both times due to his deployment
schedule. But he was now officially detached from
SEAL Team 3, ready to report to his Team 4 group at
Little Creek in five days. It didn't leave much time for a
honeymoon, so, like the wedding itself, they postponed
that too.

Last night, he'd given Aimee a gentle peck on the
cheek, knew that chances for one last encounter before
the big day, while they were both single, was out of the
question. She was buried in gifts and her girlfriends
spread over their king-sized bed. He didn't begrudge

their getting caught up. A couple of them had come a great distance to be there for her.

Eventually the magpie voices stopped, and he fell blissfully asleep, the caressing sounds of the sea in the distance. It was still there in the morning.

But this morning things were happening downstairs in the kitchen. He'd been told the caterers were coming early. The big day was upon them.

He pushed open the master bedroom door and found their vacant bed, still scattered with opened presents and remnants of wrapping paper and bows. With a glance to their closet, he noticed Aimee's green running shoes were gone and that's when he saw her leading a pack of ladies running down the beach. Even as they ran, they chattered, sparking and delighting everyone they passed by, as if the whole beach was celebrating too.

The house was half-painted on the inside. Although they'd tried to finish everything beforehand, only half the walls were covered in sheetrock. During the remodeling, they'd discovered more than the usual defects in plumbing and long-neglected air conditioning and electrical lines. Then it needed a new roof after the big storm earlier this fall, which took an unexpected chunk out of their savings since the roof had to be tied down and applied to hurricane standards. Every window, due to the storm ratings, cost three times what a normal window would cost elsewhere.

But it was their house, with creative touches and brightly colored furniture pieces they'd purchased second-hand and customized to their beach theme. Just about the only thing they didn't change was the color on the outside: *passionate Chinese red*, as Aimee called it. That had been close to the color when Aimee first spotted it a year ago.

The railing bordering the stairwell leading downstairs was made with pieces of ocean-worn branches and lumber, cut together in a hap-hazard design and then varithaned to a high polish.

Andy cinched up his pajama bottoms and skipped downstairs bare-chested and barefoot, greeting four catering staff unloading their supplies, catching a couple of the ladies off guard. One even curtsied, as if he were some prince from a foreign land.

"We've got coffee for you, Mr. Carr," said one of them.

"Thank God." He squinted and saw her nametag. "Gwen. You're a lifesaver."

She blushed and handed him a mug, but without his half and half. Before he could object, someone else brought the half gallon container over and poured easily a quarter cup into his coffee.

"Better. All's right with the world now."

"You nervous?" asked one of the cooks, beginning

to arrange plastic containers filled with appetizers. A pair of men were carrying out the folded tent for the ceremony, along with some white chairs. The florist delivered three large sprays of loose colorful flowers to be used for displays.

Andy took stock of how he felt. "Not really. I think I know what I'm getting into. We've been living together as much as we can over the past year. I'll be stationed in Little Creek now, so it will be better. Closer."

Those who looked up, gave an appreciative smile, but no one stopped to really pay any attention to him. He brought his mug outside and walked toward the water to intercept Aimee and her girlfriends.

He found them approaching from the left. He remembered the day he first saw her running on the beach in her green Nikes, how he'd been so unsure if she'd allow him to be close, and how relieved he'd been when he discovered she was softening her hard stance against him. She got closer and he studied her fresh face, her shapely form as he let her vision warm him all the way down to his toes. He was such a lucky man. He'd almost lost her, and now she would be his forever.

She was grinning at him as she attempted to run right past him, her friends in tow. He grabbed her and planted a morning kiss first on her neck, and then squarely on her lips, spilling his coffee on her in the process. Aimee jumped back to avoid additional spillage but leaned into him and gave him another quick kiss.

"You're dangerous this morning, Mr. Carr."

"I'm a lethal warrior, a force for good. Just come closer and I'll show you, Mrs. Carr."

"Not quite. Soon, but not quite."

He quickly set his mug down in the sand and ran after her as she attempted to escape. He lifted her in his arms and ran into the surf, dropping her. At the last moment, she pulled on his drawstring, bringing him crashing down into the water, his waistband slipping to expose one of his butt cheeks. The ladies howled. Andy didn't care. Wet or dry, or half-naked, he wasn't going to stop kissing her until he was good and ready to.

They made use of the long shower afterwards, in preparation for their wedding clothes, where they could be intimate in private. Her silky skin and lavender eyes begged him to be ardent, yet gentle on this special day. Her cheeks were bright pink as she came for him, as her succulent lips coaxed him on and moaned her pleasure. It was the perfect way to begin the festivities.

THE DAY WAS perfect and at sunset, they took their vows. As he kissed his new bride, his fingers slid into her hair, which had been done up with pins, flowers and miniature combs. He messed with the intricate strands and decorations, sending a couple long ringlets down her back. He got a cross look, but the audience loved it.

We winked, "You should know better by now, sweetheart. I like your hair long and sexy," he whispered.

"Thank goodness we had all the pictures taken before the ceremony," she replied, taking his hand and leading him out to the audience, who gave them a standing ovation.

He went along with the obligatory smearing of frosting on her nose and upper lip, he lovingly kissed off. He made her cry with his toast to the lovely lavender beauty who would share his life forever. Even Cory's presence couldn't dampen his day. He still didn't let him dance with Aimee, however.

His new LPO, David Peterson, came down for the occasion with two other SEALs from Team 4, a gesture Andy appreciated. He'd only had a brief workup with them and was still learning everyone's names. His former LPO, Kyle Lansdowne, had helped Andy get the job when Team 4 lost their most senior medic and was short for their next deployment.

S.O. Peterson was a much younger LPO than Kyle and had been promoted fast. Andy'd been told the heavy turnover on the team had resulted from some recent injuries and two difficult deployments in Afghanistan and Sudan, but their main arena was usually South America. It felt like the Navy was trying to find a place to stick Team 4, which was pure folly, of course. Kyle told him not to worry, that the Team was well-trained and would sync quickly around him. Andy had learned to trust Kyle's judgment on his placement, and not to ask too many questions, but it was something he thought about as the days grew closer to their deployment.

"I'm looking for great things from you, Andy," Peterson began. "Heard you're prone to heroic acts, and that's saying a bit since Team 3 is legendary for doing some pretty crazy shit," he continued as he clasped Andy's hand enough to cause a little pain.

"Most of that happened before I came on board, but we had our share. I've certainly heard the stories, sir."

"I'm counting on you to give us Africa intel. Even humanitarian security can be deadly."

Andy's personal opinion was that the African arena was more deadly than the Middle East, and certainly South America, with more groups, warring factions and less control by the governments who had been left penniless by strings of dictators who basically extracted all the country's wealth and foreign aid given to help stabilize the region. All it seemed to do was enable them to buy arms and hire mercenaries who were schooled in combating European and Africacorp troops.

Andy shook his other two teammates' hands as he answered his LPO carefully. "That's the thing. Learning who you can trust. Get that wrong, and it's all over."

The Peterson gave Andy a quick stare, laced with a dash or two of panic. Andy felt his stomach rumble, and then pushed it out of his consciousness, searching the sunset and hoping he'd have thousands more of them to come. Aimee was speaking animatedly over the laughter and happy conversation, oblivious to all this. That's exactly where he wanted her to stay.

"Got an older brother who served with a couple of your old guys, Andy. He sends his regards," said S.O. Dallas Grant, who was their explosives expert and had only eight fingers to prove it.

"You bet. He still in?"

Grant examined his toes. "There aren't too many one-armed sharpshooters on the Teams, Carr. But when I get home, he can still hunt and shoot better than I can with two arms."

The four men laughed nervously. Peterson nodded in Cory's direction. "You had your hands full there, Andy. Thanks for helping him get straight."

Andy shrugged. "We try not to leave anyone behind. We'll see. But I'd give him some space, if I were you, sir."

Peterson nodded, and then they all turned, blending into the wedding crowd. As Andy watched them disappear, he realized these guys were mere babies. He'd noticed even their senior guys, who didn't come today, were young as well. He hoped that didn't pose a problem.

Aimee's friend Shelley was all over him to dance, so he obliged her. With her silky blonde hair and good looks, this happy schoolteacher, a native of Florida, had once been his blind date when Cory was with Aimee. If Andy's bride had wanted a wedding party, Shelley would have made a stunning Maid of Honor. He knew she was still working on hooking up with a SEAL but didn't like how many times she asked for his help. He smiled anyway and gave her a thumb's up which brought on an honest blush that was kind of cute.

Thankfully, the music ended quickly, and she was called to the side. Andy went in search of his wife. He snuck up behind her, pulling her into his chest and placing a series of delicate kisses on her bare shoulder, as she cooed and dropped her conversation with a couple of her friends.

Her lavender eyes took stock of his smiling face, telling him she loved the sight of him. It was something every man needed to see, especially an elite warrior. More than words or thank yous, they needed to loom large in their lady's life. He hoped he never stopped making her pulse drive up, making her blush with his words and deeds, that she always felt safe in his arms and at his side, even when he wasn't around to reassure her. He hoped he never stopped seeing that affect he had on her. He hoped he never stopped feeling her melt as he took her for his own, whether in the middle of a crowd or in their bedroom at night. He wanted all of her, forever.

"I never want this to end, Andy," she gushed.

"It will never end, sweethcart."

"I want to keep celebrating forever." She moved her arms up, resting on his shoulders as his hands gripped her waist.

"Just being with you is a celebration, Aimee. I'm the luckiest man alive. Truly. The luckiest. You make everything beautiful."

"It's so nice we could share the magic of this place with everyone—all our friends."

"Magic." He whispered as he kissed her. "Forever."

"The magic will bring you home to me," she answered with a sigh. "It will pull you back here, to the Gulf."

"No, you pull me back here. Because this is where you are."

"And I'll always be on the beach waiting for you, or running, or eating pancakes, until you come home again."

He pressed his forehead against hers and hoped he wasn't showing his apprehension for the new deployment and the new team. That warm glow where Aimee lived in his heart expanded inside his chest and eclipsed his worries.

Nothing would interfere with his perfect day.

CHAPTER 3

Christmas Day

AIMEE FINGERED THE ribbons on several of the packages that remained unopened from the reception last night at sunset. The barefoot beach wedding had been perfect. It was ordered that no one wore shoes so dancing in the sand in her long wedding gown was a challenge, and her calves and thighs were paying the price for her fun. But long after the orange glow of the dying sun had disappeared, the glow in her heart remained.

All of a sudden, her eyes teared up, impeding her from being able to read the card from one of the gifts. Wiping her eyes, she decided some coffee might help. Her belly gurgled—the lack of sleep their lovemaking had caused was just another happy consequence of being so madly, hopelessly in love. She floated to the kitchen, turned water on the stove, scooped coffee into the French press and waited for her pot to boil.

She heard Andy's footsteps on the stairs.

His sinfully god-like body was bare-chested. He wore his brand-new Christmas boxers she'd given him last night. She hoped she looked half as good as he did this morning.

"Morning, Mrs. Carr," he said, pinning her against the refrigerator and planting a long languid kiss on her caffeine-starved lips.

"Good morning yourself, Mr. Carr. I didn't expect you to be up and awake before noon, knowing how you like your beauty rest."

"The bed was empty and cold. Can't sleep when it's that way. You slipped out rather stealth, my dear. What is your secret mission?"

"Coffee." She poured the boiling water into the carafe while she foraged for half and half in the packed refrigerator. "I'm hoping someone comes over today. There's so much food here, we could feed everyone on the beach all day long."

"Not a bad idea," Andy said as he accepted the cream she poured into his favorite Navy SEAL mug. He poured coffee for both of them and followed her to the living room couch with a view of the sugary white sand beach and the new day beyond.

Aimee would go for a run later, but right now, it just felt good to be lazy on the couch with the fresh coffee and her handsome new husband. She wrapped herself tighter in her robe, tucked her legs under her and sipped, watching Andy's Adam's apple move deliciously up and down as he swallowed his coffee.

He pointed to the table still covered with gifts. "Should I bring some of these over so we can finish opening them?"

Aimee yawned before she could say a thing, which caused her to start laughing when Andy noticed the lack of sleep was affecting her. She took another sip, and then sighed. "I like just sitting here next to you right now. I'm beginning to wonder if this coffee is going to do its thing. What did we get, two, maybe three hours of sleep last night?"

Andy wiggled his eyebrows. "Less than that, I think. But who's counting." He slipped his hand inside her robe and gently caressed her right breast. His coffee was precariously held in his other hand.

"Careful, Andy. You're deadly with the coffee spills…"

"I just get distracted." He shifted his weight closer to her and adjusted his crotch.

She took his mug, holding them both up in the air while Andy licked and fondled both her breasts, which were spread open for him. The familiar ache for him brought fine beads of perspiration to her upper lip while she watched his head reach lower as his tongue traveled to her belly button. When he came up for air, his eyes were deep navy blue, his lips begged to be kissed. He quickly removed the coffee impediment, slipped down his boxers, revealing how ready he was, and pressed her gently back onto the leather couch.

"Oh, Mrs. Carr, I could get used to this," he whispered in her ear as he slipped inside her. The leather couch groaned as he maneuvered his hips back and forth, his hand gently pressing on her rear, pushing her up into him deeper.

But Aimee couldn't think of anything to say, except, "Yessss."

AFTER BREAKFAST, SHE started to go over the gifts again. She brought three over to the couch as Andy joined her. He took the card, opened it, and read, "From Jasper Kornblum, Esq." Andy said, holding up his card. "Hope you have a century of happiness here together."

"That's Carmen's attorney. I didn't see him at the reception, but he must have come."

She tore open the light silver wrapping paper covering a large white box.

"I talked to him a few minutes. He's a nice old guy. I usually don't like attorneys."

"Me neither. Necessary evil," she answered, pulling a crystal bowl out from tissue and bubble wrap inside the box. "This is gorgeous. Perfect fruit bowl. Waterford. Expensive." She held the cut crystal up to the light. Tiny chards of rainbows radiated all over the walls of the living room and above.

"Very nice. I didn't know you invited him," said Andy, taking the bowl from her fingers and placing it on the gift table.

"I sent one to Carmen Hernandez, his client. I didn't expect her to come or to send him. I just wanted her to know we were getting married here. This house meant so much to her, or so we were told."

"But this is from him, not her, right?" asked Andy.

"Well, I'd say she already gave us a gift. She agreed to sell us this house. Maybe we could visit her sometime."

Andy gathered up the wrapping paper and packing, and then took a seat next to Aimee. "From the sounds of it, she's not doing too well. You'd better go while I'm overseas because he said she didn't have long."

"That's too bad. Of course. I'll do that. What else did he say?"

"He said he'd be calling on us soon, that he had some papers he wanted to discuss, when the time came. Kind of a cryptic answer, if you ask me."

"Oh Geez, I hope nothing is wrong with the title."

"You got insurance, though, right?"

"I did."

"Well, we should be okay then. He didn't look like it was a problem, just wanted to pay his respects and to tell us he'd be in touch. I kind of like the guy."

Andy found it easy to like almost anybody, Aimee noted to herself. But he also was a good judge of character, and if there was some malicious intent, Andy would have picked up on it right away.

They continued opening up packages. Aimee was careful to add these to her list for thank you notes.

A brief knock on the door startled them both. Andy ran over and waved at the departing delivery truck driver who had just dropped a box on their doorstep.

"On Christmas Day?" Aimee was shocked. "Who is it from?"

Andy squinted at the label. "Della Fortunati. It's from Nashville." He held the box up and shrugged.

"Oh, she was my agent when I sold my parent's home there. How lovely. And for the record, I didn't invite her."

"Well, it's still nice. Here." He handed the preprinted delivery box to her, and then retrieved a pair of scissors from the kitchen so she could get past all the plastic tape covering nearly every square inch of the box.

Aimee sliced through the seams and opened the flaps. Inside was a note.

Aimee,

The Andersons found these upstairs in the attic of your mother's home. Somehow, when you and

I were cleaning everything out, we missed this. Sorry. But I took a brief look at it and knew these things you'd want to have.

—Della

Beneath the note were several stacks of old pictures of their family. Aimee was fascinated to examine the ones when she and Logan were grade school age. Her parents looked so young then. There were a couple of her report cards, a Father's Day drawing she'd made, a Christmas ornament Logan had made, and some folded papers, including Aimee's birth certificate.

"This is really cool, Andy. I've never seen some of these."

"How nice they forwarded them on. Now I know you won't be bored when I'm gone. These will take you two days to go through, if I know you well enough."

Aimee was overjoyed and didn't know where to start looking through everything. She was tickled that part of her family history, which had scattered after the death of her parents and the disappearance of her brother Logan, was chronicled here. Intact. Preserved just for her. Examining one photo of Logan in a basketball jersey, a tall, skinny kid with a big smile, he didn't resemble the troubled young man who was now living on the streets, battling his addiction demons. She was grateful for the hand-up. This gave her more impetus to go looking for him again.

She handed the box to Andy, who was frowning as he placed it on the table. Aimee opened another package.

Over dinner, Andy had been quiet. Aimee thought perhaps the three plus short days they had left was beginning to get to him, so she didn't want to put any attention on it and hoped it would just pass. But the longer it went on, no matter how many times she tried to engage Andy in light conversation, he was guarded. It wasn't something she was used to. She'd finally decided to bring it up, and then he began to speak.

"Aimee, we're always supposed to have this talk with our wives and parents before deployment. Just so you know, they had me write a letter to you, and, if something happens, you'll get it."

"Andy, don't. Can't we wait a couple of days to talk about this?"

"I was going to. But these photographs you were sent got me thinking."

"Okay."

"We weren't married before when I went off, so I didn't prepare you well enough. That's on me. And you know life is fragile. We never know if we might step into something totally unforeseen, even with all the best planning and intel. So, you know the drill. Something happens to me, you go on, and you try, if you can, to pick another Team guy. And they'll be coming too."

"Andy, I've been told this. Christy had a good talk with me last time. I really don't want to go into it right now."

"Just hear me out and then you can be mad, if you want to. It's about what you do when I'm out of the US. You watch for odd things, people who get interested in you. Be careful of what you say to others, especially about me, or anything about what I do for a living."

"I know this."

"And you stick with the wives you know, even though they won't have husbands who are deployed. My new LPO is not much older than I am, and I haven't met his wife, but they are newly married. Help her out, if you can, because she's no Christy Lansdowne."

"I will. You'll leave contact information?"

"Yes, we have a sheet with the other names to stay in touch with, like a phone tree, but you have the old Team 3 guys and gals, so use them too."

"I will." Aimee could see there was still something else.

"I hesitated to bring this up, but I want you to hear me on this, Aimee." Andy took her hands in his, and, across the table, squeezed them. "About looking for Logan. I'm going to ask you not to go doing that."

"Why?"

"Because it's dangerous. He might be dangerous. He might be hanging with dangerous people. You have to take extra precautions to be safe, okay?"

"But I'm not going to be searching through homeless shelters or walking the streets, Andy. I might want to check in with the clinic where he was staying, you know, talk to his old doctor."

"He said he'd contact you if he heard anything. But please, don't go anywhere or do anything on your own that could possibly put yourself in danger. And it's not because I don't think you're savvy and smart. I just won't be here to jump in if it was needed. You never know with these kinds of things." He squeezed her hands again. "Like I said earlier, life is fragile."

Her eyes were watering as she began to see how concerned he was for her safety. The reality that they'd be separated for what could be several months began to dawn on her. She was missing him already. But she also didn't know how to reassure him that she'd be smart, and she'd be safe.

"Andy, I love you for caring about my safety. I really do. But don't worry. I won't do anything stupid or anything that would put myself in any danger."

"You remember what the doctor said. He told you not to go looking for Logan. He even said it wasn't safe. If you saw him, not to expect that he'd be well enough to have interaction without you being in danger. Remember, honey?"

Aimee had fought the doctor's words that day just as she was fighting Andy's words now. But she didn't want him to worry, even though she knew nothing would ever stop her from looking for her brother. She didn't want Andy leaving with that concern. She didn't want to lie, either.

"I promise to be safe, Andy. Thank you for reminding me. I'll be smart. You'll see. No worries there."

"So, you'll give me your word you won't go on a scavenger hunt for Logan?"

She hesitated just long enough to cause Andy to give a worried sigh.

"Aimee, I have to have your word. Especially no streaking out on your own."

"I promise. If the doctor calls me, I'll bring Shelley. If I run into Logan, which I don't think I will, but if I do, I won't try to approach him."

"Because you tried to before, remember?"

"Yes, I know. I won't do that again."

"Okay, sweetheart. Thank you. Please, do this for me."

"I will. I promise. You have to promise to come back to me all in one piece, okay?"

"Remember the magic. The magic will bring me home. You'll see."

CHAPTER 4

THE SEPARATION FROM Aimee was more difficult than Andy expected—for him. Aimee cried, but held herself together when he denied her request to travel to Little Creek to see him off. He'd told her it was part of his concern that she not take long trips alone, at least until he was back in the States. He promised her the mission was expected to only take sixty days, which was a bit of a white lie, since it was more than possible it could extend another two to four months.

He figured that was the source of his upset, and like he always did on missions, got himself into game mode, like he'd been trained. Lots of things happened at home when they were gone. This was just a little trip, a little lie, he told himself.

He'd started making a list of things he'd have to pick up at the Team building, since the Gulf Coast wasn't exactly the place he could obtain gear for the trip. He'd gotten his Africa shots some six months ago when he deployed with Team 3. He was relieved that he wouldn't have those sore arms as he bounced around in transport planes on the way over. On top of everything else, he was grateful for this little break.

But the days went by quickly and the two of them did half of what they'd planned on doing before his leaving. Of course, that was partly his fault, since they did spend a lot of time in the bedroom, not that Aimee minded. He didn't think getting married would make him feel differently about having sex with her, but it did. This time it was serious. They were a forever couple, not just dating or even living together. He reveled in the celebration of their vows and their love every time he thought about that day. Just like the first day he met her in Cory's rented bungalow, he knew she'd be a part of his life in the future. Now he had all her future, as long as he did his job and came back safe.

And maybe that's why it was harder for him to leave. He had more to lose. He'd become a SEAL as a dumb single guy obsessed with equipment, gear, dangerous stuff, things he could fix and things he could blow up. Having Aimee in his life eclipsed them all.

The long good-bye kiss was over. He stood nervously in front of her silently weeping form. "Hey, it's going to be okay. Just keep close to the wives," he whispered to the top of her head. "And, get some sleep."

She chuckled into his chest. The tension was gone.

He placed his fingers over her lips so she wouldn't say good-bye, which was a rule for him, gave her a wink, and hopped into his truck for the twelve hour drive up north that would take him all night long. As he backed out the driveway into the beach trail road, he reminded her, "I'll call you before I take off, sweetheart."

He waved and watched her wave in response through his rearview mirror.

Gulf Boulevard was bathed in that familiar orange glow. He stopped several times to make way for groups of beachgoers who had crossed the road originally to stand at the surf's edge, some with cooler wagons, umbrellas and folded beach chairs in tow.

This was the end of the year already! An unusually warm December. When a third of the country was under a blanket of snow and howling winds. Andy thought it was fitting to leave Sunset Beach at this time of day, with the warm sun and ocean breeze in his face.

The time of magic. He knew it would still be there when he returned.

ANDY ARRIVED AT base just as the sun was reappearing. The first thing he noticed was the frigid temperature. Anywhere else but Florida, December would be one of the coldest months. He missed his

Hawaiian trunks and flip flops already. He was going to pick up another heavy water-resistant jacket for the trip over, since sometimes the transports were drafty, and they usually flew at night. December was one of West Africa's warmer and wettest months.

He reported to the Team building, one of the first to arrive. Peterson greeted him with a warm handshake. "Happy to see you, Andy. I knew I didn't have to worry, but I wouldn't have blamed you if you went AWOL on me. New bride, beautiful beaches. Nice warm weather." He shook his head, suddenly at a loss for words.

"Nah, and miss all the fun in Africa? The bugs and snakes the size of a VW bus and that red clay that stalls anything within a hundred feet? No way, man."

Peterson took it well and slapped him on the back. "You're right. We were made for this shit, weren't we?"

"Hell yeah!" Andy noted the charts and maps laid out for his presentation later in the morning. "Looks like you're finishing your homework. I'll let you to it, then."

"I'm thinking you drove straight through. Am I right?" he asked Andy.

"Yessir. I did."

"So, you go over there where we've got a couple cots and some blankets. The showers are in the corner as well if you want to freshen up. We're starting at nine hundred, so you got about two hours to yourself. Can't promise breakfast, but something's coming just before, if you're hungry. Or, you can run over to Beck Hall for some grub."

Andy weighed the value of a shower against getting some rest, something to eat or a new jacket. He decided he could make do without the breakfast and maybe bum a jacket off another Team Guy. "Thanks, I think I'll just do that."

He ambled over to the dark corner, tossed his bag on a folded pile of blankets, snatched a fresh tee shirt and shorts from his bag, collected his shave kit and headed to the showers.

In five minute's time he had completed his triple S routine and tucked himself between two scratchy brown blankets, finding the oversized cot a perfect fit. He pretended the blowers up in the roof rafters were ocean sounds and was hard asleep in seconds.

Mumbled conversation and a latrine flushing woke him up. In the shadows, he quickly donned his jeans and a long-sleeved flannel shirt, straightened his gear and walked into the lighted room filled with about twenty Team Guys. He shook hands with Archie Nolan and Dallas Grant, who had accompanied his LPO to his wedding.

Dallas pointed to a tray of bagels and cream cheese, fresh fruit and coffee nearby. "Grab some fixin's, if you're hungry."

As he made his way back to a seat next to Dallas and Archie, Peterson began his presentation. The lights dimmed, as a map of Nigeria and the surrounding area came into view on a large screen.

"This is going to be my first trip to West Africa, but some of you who have come from other teams, like Andy, here, are more familiar with the geography and people. We've seen some major instability in both Nigeria and Benin over the past few years, and heavy violence erupted last year which required Uncle Sam's help, some of it heavy and seen, and some unseen. And there are some bigger players on the horizon destabiliz-ing the area."

Andy had heard it before. He'd seen first-hand the destruction left behind by local militia groups who had formed in the vacuum created by governments who were unable to exert peaceful control over the region. It's what made this part of the world so dangerous. New militia groups, along with leaders with grand plans of country domination and asset control, were popping up all the time, their loyalties sometimes murky.

"We've got a group of Western journalists and aid workers being held captive by a small army that crossed into Nigeria earlier this month, but they are aligned with a rebel leader in Benin who is launching opposition to the duly elected President. We aren't interested in the politics. We don't care who these groups are, except that we have to find a way to get our American aid workers and two Dutch journalists out without creating an outright civil war."

Peterson didn't give anyone time to react. It didn't take many words to paint the picture of what a mess the factions had made of two countries and threatening to be a powder keg to draw in several others.

"Most of these militias are fighters from neighboring countries who are just trying to make a few bucks to send home to their families, anyway. Freelancers. So, there's no real political agenda here, and not a real religious or ethnic one, either, which is a shame. Benin is one of the oldest independent nations in Africa and once had a flourishing democracy until recently."

Peterson scanned the room, and then continued. "We think there are still six people, four males and two females, being held. We aren't sure about their physical condition, either, but reports say so far, they are uninjured, but no doubt suffering at the hands of the guards. No ransom demands are being made. They are a grass roots and not well funded missionary group from the Pacific Northwest, part of a megachurch ministry and had no business being there. But we don't always get the smart ones. They do require rescuing and State has pushed us to act."

Andy was intrigued by the Dutch journalists, so he raised his hand.

"Andy?"

"Sir, the journalists. What publication are they from?"

"From what we've been able to make out they were along for the publicity, recording with a camera crew, all the good works the aid workers were doing. They brought a ton of bibles to hand out, all sponsored by a huge church fellowship. It was to be for some documentary coming up. But we don't really know, Andy."

"You have a reason for asking?" Dallas Grant barked, even though he was sitting right next to Andy.

"Well, we uncovered elements of human smuggling in the Canaries and at Cape Verde on Team 3. I wasn't on all those missions, but we did nab a couple of Dutchmen who were involved in some heavy trafficking of young girls. They had a ring that extended well into Nigeria."

"I imagine State is looking into that," said Peterson. "If you have contacts, help me out, Andy. One of the issues here is that everyone works together for a bit, and then they're all for themselves and they go to war and resurface somewhere else. It's a revolving door."

Andy completely agreed.

Peterson outlined some logistics of the trip over, and indicated they'd be leaving at dusk so that they'd have the cover of darkness when they landed at a recently fortified base created in neighboring Niger.

When the meeting broke up, he asked Dallas Grant, who was about Andy's size, if he had an extra jacket he could borrow for the trip. Dallas led him over to his duty locker and pulled out a bag with a brand-new Trident Concept water-repellant jacked with all the zipper pockets and compartments a frog could ever want. Before he handed it to Andy, Dallas pulled the tags off.

"I can't take this. It's way too nice, and it's brand new."

"Sure you can. I haven't had time to customize it, and it will drive me crazy if I can't reach my gear quickly when we're in the field. You take it. I can get another one when I get back."

"I'm paying for it, though."

"If you insist," Dallas said, shrugging his shoulders.

"Thanks, man. I'm seriously stoked."

"Well, don't complain if the zippers are stiff, or the angle is wrong for your hands. I gotta get my stash without thinking too much about it. You might want to shoot me later."

"Not a chance. I'll bring a needle and thread and work on it when we arrive if we have time."

"Okay by me, Dolly Madison. Say, if you're good to go, wanna grab a burger? It will be a long time before we'll see anything that fat and juicy again, trust me."

"McCoy's? Cory used to rave about it all the time!"

"Yup. All the bacon and avocados and horseradish you can stand. Of course, in Cory's case, we had to limit the beer and other stuff, but the two of us spent quite a lot of time getting our carb load back when he was here."

"Done deal. Say no more, but you better drive. I'm all turned around."

Before they left the building, Andy gave Peterson a couple of names.

"If you have time, Kyle can get you those numbers. You'll want to talk to them."

"I'm all over this. I've heard of this Sven guy. You deployed with him?"

"Former Norwegian FSK. You won't get a better guide. And, last I checked, the two of them are kind of an item, but you didn't hear it from me. Kelly has good instincts."

"Thanks. I'm calling him now."

Dallas inserted himself. "Excuse me, Peterson, want us to bring you back a burger?"

"Now why in the Hell would I turn that down? Thanks." He started to dig into his back pocket and Dallas stopped him.

"We'll catch you when we get back."

Both Cory and Dallas had been right. Even though

Andy knew he'd be comatose in an hour, the burger was everything he'd hoped for. He relished getting catsup all over his chin, which he cleanly wiped off. Inside of five days, he'd have a full beard. The fries were hand cut and gigantic wedges smothered in barbeque and rock salt. They each washed it down with a draft, which wasn't exactly regulation, but Andy knew it would help him catch a little more shuteye before the boarding.

"How is Cory doing, anyhow? I tried to talk to him at the wedding, but he wasn't having it," posed Dallas. "And I didn't want to ask in front of our LPO."

"He's working things out, or says he is. I keep my eye on him a bit, especially around Aimee."

"Fuck yeah."

"He sort of avoids me too. But he told me he'd stopped drinking, so, I'm hoping that's the case. Haven't seen him acting out much. He'll always be over the top. But you know how the Navy is about injuries, so I suspect he's headed for a drop. I hope not, though."

"Yeah. That would be a shame. Hellofa fun guy, though. Just would never trust him with my daughter—if I had one!"

Back at the team building, Dallas brought Peterson's burger and onion rings and the two of them headed for the back corner. Andy checked his phone and didn't see a message from Aimee, so laid back and covered his eyes and forehead with the backside of his old Fresno State baseball cap as Dallas hunkered down on the cot adjacent, after putting in his ear pods.

Several hours later, as the Team walked across the tarmac to the waiting transport, Andy pulled out his cell and dialed Aimee.

"Hey you."

"Hey yourself," Andy said as he kept walking. "Can you hear me?"

"Not real well. Would you mind asking the pilot to turn off those engines I hear in the background?"

"Cute. I don't want to get on his bad side or he's liable to drop me over the Atlantic."

"Good thinking. So, you're about to board?"

"Yup."

"And are you going to some place familiar?"

She was clever with the light interrogation.

"God no," he lied. He hoped this wasn't going to start becoming a habit. But security on their cell phones had been drilled into them, and Aimee should have known better. He told himself she'd asked for it. "Still, not a safe place. I'll tell you all about the beaches when I get back home."

"You're lying."

"I'm not telling." He loved their banter. "So, sweetheart, do me a favor and take off all your clothes right now."

"I'm almost naked. In my underwear."

"Well, definitely take off those panties, then. You don't need them. I want you sleeping butt naked in my bed tonight."

"Our bed, handsome."

"On second thought, maybe I could bribe this guy to fly me back to Florida. What do you say?"

"In your dreams, cowboy."

"I'd take a ride. A nice slow one, right about now."

"And we could take turns who's on top. I'm all rested. Frisky as Hell."

"I'm getting the message loud and clear. I'm not going to be able to sit down in a couple seconds."

"Awww. Poor baby. I have a cure for that."

"You do. You definitely do. So, hold that thought. Stay safe. Keep the doors and windows locked. And when I get home, plan on not wearing a stitch for at least a couple of weeks, okay?"

"It's a deal. I can't wait. And let the magic pull you back, Andy. I need you here. Now and always."

"Same thing sweetheart. Love you forever."

"Forever it is. I'll be waiting. Naked."

CHAPTER 5

THE NEXT MORNING, Aimee dressed and put on her running shoes and made it to the beach before her mood and her will changed. She knew the physical exercise would do her good and she wasn't wrong.

It was a bit foggy this morning, unlike the several days prior, which were exceptionally clear and warm. The old fisherman was already out in his lawn chair, his windbreaker pulled tight around his body and the hood tied with a black cord framing his reddened face. He was already working on a beer. His pole was secured in the plastic stake dug a foot deep in the semi-wet sand as he watched the tip for a bob or tug. The line going out into the surf was taut, waiting to snag something that could go into his blue plastic bucket that was bigger than the bait he kept swimming there.

He was a regular and Aimee suspected he ate fish for breakfast nearly every morning.

"Morning," she said as she passed him.

"God Bless. You have a good day now," he answered.

Two ladies rode motorized fat tire bicycles and followed the shore in tandem, chattering away, waving to her and then going right back to their animated conversation. Another group of young couples ran in a pod of a dozen or so at a pretty good clip. Aimee focused on the smooth stretch of beach ahead and didn't pay them much attention. She wasn't there to make friends and didn't need the distraction.

She was thinking about the pictures and other treasures in the box that had been left on Christmas Day. It was a snapshot into her parent's life when things were happy, before Logan disappeared. She had spent late into the night searching all their faces as if she could determine what had happened to change their family dynamic so. But she came away with nothing. The wide smiles and affectionate poses belied the future that would engulf them all in sorrow.

The mystery of her family was more than just Logan and his mental illness. There was something else there, she thought, as she flipped through the pictures. But she couldn't put her finger on it.

Her timer on her watch went off. She turned and headed back home.

After her shower, she made a smoothie and sat watching the ocean while she drank her breakfast and dried her hair with a towel. A silver flash of the crystal bowl caught her eye and she retrieved the attorney's card and her cell phone, dialing.

Kornblum's secretary answered in a sweet voice and let Aimee know he wasn't expected in the office until this afternoon. She left her phone number for a return call.

Pulling out her beach-themed thank you notes, she began composing a message to the older attorney, thanking him for the beautiful bowl, adding how the cutting in the crystal sides lit up the room in color and light.

She sat back and looked at her note.

"Kind of dumb," she murmured. "Too girly for him," she continued. She was going to rip it up and start again when she changed her mind and decided to embellish it instead.

We've always loved how the sun bounces off the walls of this house, spreading different colors, depending on the time of day. This lovely piece of crystal will be well used and goes so perfectly with the magic and drama we find here. We call it our magic.

She smiled. It was kind of corny, but she decided to send it anyway. Labeling the envelope with the information from the card, she placed her heart stamp on the outside, sealed it, and placed it on the small table by the front door to mail.

Aimee kept her grandmother's old desk in the corner of her bedroom. She pulled down the front partition, revealing cubbies stuffed with little keepsakes and office supplies she'd gathered. She even had some old paperclips and labels that had to be licked, curled and yellowed in their original boxes. As a child, she remembered how fascinated she was to explore all these simple treasures and was often scolded for not leaving her things alone.

This morning, she pulled out the brown envelope that held a copy of her title papers, and a copy of the life estate that had been created for the previous owner. Somewhere she'd written down the name of the complex where Mrs. Hernandez resided in Sarasota. She found it written in the lower right corner of the letter from Mr. Kornblum, effectively accepting her verbal offer to purchase the house, and outlining the terms of the sale.

Our Lady of Light.

She loved the name. Most things in Florida were named after palm trees, or ocean breezes with words like *paradise* sprinkled in the middle. But Our Lady of Light was distinctly different. The previous owner might have chosen it because of the name.

She searched her phone for a phone number and dialed it.

"May I speak to one of your residents, a Carmen

Hernandez, please?"

"Miss Hernandez is in the critical care wing of our facility and she does not take phone calls. I'm sorry. Are you a relative?"

"No, a family friend. What are visiting hours?"

"I'm afraid you'll have to get the family's permission to see her. Let me put you through to the other side."

Without asking for approval, Aimee was placed on hold. A male attendant answered the phone next.

"Can I help you?"

"I'm wanting to visit Mrs. Carmen Hernandez. How do I make an appointment?" she asked.

"Are you family?"

"Family friend. She knows me through correspondence."

"I'm afraid you'll need family permission to see her. None of our patients here are allowed visitors unless with a family member."

"I see." Aimee knew she wouldn't get a satisfactory answer, but she had to ask the question anyway. "How is she doing?"

"We can't give that information out."

"But is she getting stronger, better, or—"

"Generally, this facility is end of life care. It's mostly hospice patients here. Miss Hernandez is in that category, which is all I can tell you. She has good days and bad days—I think you can read between the lines."

"Yes, thank you."

She inhaled to avoid the flood of tears that were threatening. She was overwhelmed with sadness that she hadn't thought to visit the woman before now. Perhaps it was too late. Aimee was filled with regret.

She picked up the life estate document, bound in a dark brown book cover. She skimmed over the boiler plate until she came to more of the meat of the document.

*I, Hank Borges, bequeath my sole separate property to Miss Carmen Hernandez for as long as she shall live, along with a stipend of...*It was several thousand dollars a month he had provided for her. As Aimee read on, she discovered the home was delivered to her free and clear, without a mortgage, and that a maintenance fund was set up for care of the landscaping and for repairs as required. That struck Aimee as odd, since the house had fallen into such disrepair when she found it a year ago.

What happened? Who was Hank Borges? The name was slightly familiar to Aimee, but she couldn't pinpoint why.

She got out her laptop and looked up Hank Borges, resident of Sunset Beach but formerly from Manhattan. His biography was short. His obituary from 1998 was long.

Popular science fiction author of some eighty novels made famous by such motion pictures as the Red Planet and The Soul of The Moon, she read.

There was a picture taken of him on a sunny day, the wind blowing through his nearly white hair, with the unmistakable backdrop of a white sand beach and ocean in the background. Aimee wondered if it was taken here, at this very house, but the detail was slightly fuzzy and hard to make out.

So, Hank Borges perhaps had lived here at one time too. Were they married? If so, why did the attendant call her Miss Hernandez?

Aimee read further about his life in New York, and a notation that he'd become even more prolific when he retired and moved to the Florida Gulf Coast, which had always been his writing inspiration. He had doubled his production of books and was in the middle of finishing a novel on the day of his death at seventy-two.

But there wasn't any mention of a Carmen Hernandez, or a wife or companion. And maybe, she thought, that was what he wanted. Perhaps that was their silent arrangement.

Now Aimee was intrigued and even more upset with herself for perhaps missing the chance to meet this mystery woman, who obviously meant something to the famous author.

She knew Kornblum would have the answers she sought.

Aimee took the sheets off the bed and ran several loads of laundry while she toyed with the idea of driving down to Sarasota to see if she could somehow sneak in an audience with the elderly lady who used to own this home.

She was vacuuming and nearly didn't hear her phone ring in time. Jasper Kornblum had returned her call.

"I'm glad you like the bowl. My wife is much better at picking out wedding gifts, so I'm afraid I can't take any credit for it. She has nice tastes."

"Oh, I'm sorry I missed her as well."

"No, no. I came alone. I just was curious to see what you'd done with the place so I could report to Carmen. We didn't want to impose."

"You totally could have brought her. I wish you had. We had plenty, as I'm sure you saw."

"It was a perfect day for the perfect couple." He cleared his throat. "So, what can I do for you?"

"Andy has just left for overseas. But I was wondering if I could arrange a meeting with Mrs.

Hernandez—"

"*Miss* Hernandez. She never married."

"Right. Well, Andy said you told him she's not doing very well. I'm afraid I neglected to reach out before, but I wanted to thank her for letting us buy the house. I took the liberty of calling Our Lady of Light and they've told me I have to be family. Can you arrange a meeting?"

"She's not going to recover, Aimee. Between you and me, her demise could happen any day now."

"Then all the more reason to try to see her sooner. Can you authorize this?"

"I can, but I won't unless her doctor says it wouldn't be too risky. She's very frail. Everything is being done to keep her comfortable, but she sleeps most of the day. Let me see if I can reach him, and then I'll let you know. What's your schedule like?"

"I'm open. My primary job is to do some painting, coordinate workmen we've scheduled. I could be available anytime, really."

"Okay, little lady. Let me see what I can arrange. I'm sure she'd want to meet you. But, unfortunately, she might not even know you're there. I saw her two weeks ago and was surprised how far down she had gone. But she's a fighter. I'll ring you back as soon as I find out, okay?"

"Thank you, Mr. Kornblum. You have a nice day."

"You as well, Aimee."

After he hung up, Aimee was disappointed she hadn't asked about Hank Borges. She made a mental note to do so the next conversation.

On the internet, she looked up Mr. Borges' books, and found most of them out of print, but several copies were available used. She ordered three and saw that they'd be arriving in just two days.

Just before dinner she received the call she'd been hoping for. Jasper Kornblum agreed to pick her up in the morning and drive her himself to Sarasota where they might be able to visit Miss Hernandez. He cautioned her about getting too excited for much conversation.

Aimee knew it was going to be hard getting herself to sleep tonight. She couldn't wait for her new adventure.

But before she drifted off, she said a little prayer for Andy on the other side of the world somewhere. Her evenings meant his day was just beginning.

She sent a little magic his way.

CHAPTER 6

THE LANDING WAS far from perfect, and the fact that there were so many potholes in the hastily created landing strip set out in the middle of rural Niger, the entire team sighed in relief when at last the engines were cut and their forward bumpy momentum stopped.

Peterson stood at the doorway, which had to be unsecured. He banged on the steel frame several times and then Andy heard the distinctive whir and buzz-buzz of the electric drill removing all the rivets securing the door.

The blast of hot hair and the smell of swamp overwhelmed them all, even though it was still before sunrise. Several coughed. Andy pulled his bandana up over his nose and mouth, turned his baseball cap backwards and unzipped his jacket. In a matter of minutes, he'd be roasting like a hot dog in a bun, but now wasn't the time to strip down and perhaps overlook some of his gear.

Peterson had jumped from the plane nearly four feet and sorely complained.

"Holy shit storm assignment from Hell."

Their LPO's words set Andy's nerves on edge. He was used to Kyle's swearing on missions, but not first jump out of the gate. He read no humor in the faces of all the men on the team who waited their turn to exit the transport. An uneasy lull fell over the crowd.

Several voices in an African dialect Andy didn't recognize chattered orders and recommendations as a stairway was dragged to the opening for everyone else to use. It had four wheels attached to it, but one of them was missing, so the action required four strong men to position.

Andy was familiar with the sunglass-encased stern faces dressed in khaki fatigues that many of the African and Coalition-trained forces wore. Smiles were very expensive and usually not trusted. He got the vibe right away that pissing contests were to be avoided, if they valued their life. It was never lost on him that he was a guest in someone else's country, and the presence of a SEAL platoon wasn't always good news for the locals. The alliances were complicated and far too complex for him to understand and, as Peterson said, this wasn't about politics. As long as the rental fees, for the privilege of conducting some kind of operation here were paid, all was well. Everything had a price. Even free wasn't.

And all of it was totally out of their control. They had to trust the system that sometimes got it horribly wrong. This one had been feeling this way to Andy since the moment they left the base in Virginia.

They heard a diesel bus drone in the distance, with two yellowing headlights moving toward them. Another four-door Russian-made Humvee type vehicle followed behind. As the rear taillights on the bus flashed, Andy could see that the other vehicle was missing a door. It seemed anything that came in fours was missing something. A wheel here, a door there. As long as it wasn't too important, they'd have to live with things like this. He guessed some local leader had needed that door more than the militia group did.

Peterson and two of the other Team guys were instructed to go with the driver in the truck, while everyone else piled into the bus. Andy was pleasantly surprised at the cleanliness of the insides, with the exception of a rear bathroom, again without a door, which seemed to be a common theme again, and stunk like a dead animal. Everyone avoided the rear as much as possible. Windows were opened, those that worked, anyhow. The men kept their masks on not for sanitation, but to avoid the noxious smell.

Andy took a seat by himself and Dallas took the

one behind him, resting their packs beside them. Dallas managed to finally get the window between them open to a four-inch crack as the diesel engine kicked in and a cloud of black smoke was visible out the rear window as they pulled away. They watched as their LPO struck out ahead, disappearing in the low-lying bushes on a well-worn trail that could almost be called a road, just as their transport quickly turned the opposite direction and took off into the night sky.

Their leader's truck was probably easier to see through the red clay dust billowing behind them because of the brake lights. The road was relatively smooth, and straight, which alleviated one of Andy's fears of maneuverability. The driver ground the gears frequently and didn't appear to be very experienced overcorrecting to avoid potholes and occasionally a long-dead animal.

He glanced at Dallas, checking his phone. The screen illuminated his face and beard that was new since the wedding. Andy's would be matching him in about as much time.

"Get anything?" he asked.

"Nothing I trust." Dallas flipped off the phone. "Probably shouldn't have fired it up, but I just wanted to know how isolated we are," he added.

"Wanna take turns with trying to catch few more Z's?" Andy asked him.

"No, you go ahead. I'm good. My nerves are fried. Every trip to Africa it gets worse. I hate this place, truth be told," he whispered.

Andy nodded his complete understanding. When he'd agreed to sign on to Team 4, he had hoped that Africa wasn't going to be one of the destinations. "Crude and bumpy as it is, way better to come this way than do a drop. The way this place changes almost daily, no telling where it's safe, even if you embed with locals. I'm sure I don't have to tell you that, Dallas."

"No, you're right. That's how we lost our medic in Venezuela on that evacuation. The whole thing went to shit after that."

"Was Cory with you guys then?"

"Nope, that was the time before. That one didn't turn out so well either." Dallas leaned over the seat and was very careful with his whisper, coming close enough to Andy's ear he could feel his Teammate's hot breath. "I'm beginning to think #4 is my unlucky number. At least for this crew it is. Half this group is trying to transfer out."

Andy's bowels nearly gave way. This was not what he wanted to hear. He'd heard talk about how some Teams just didn't gel well. Often times a change in leadership was required before anyone developed the confidence in each other they required to be able to work as one cohesive unit. He wondered if the young

LPO was that impediment.

But now wasn't the time to be second-guessing his new leader, either.

"I think Peterson's okay, Dallas. Doesn't help when the team is being shoved all over the globe."

"He shouldn't have told the guys it was his first trip."

"We aren't stupid. Everyone would have figured it out. I think he's okay. Besides, you're scaring me and now I won't be able to sleep either. So, knock it off."

"Yeah, I do that sometimes. Apologies. We just need some cohesive muscle memory and then we'll be fine. But if the leader doesn't lead, that's how mistakes happen when other people try to step up to fill the void. I think he's a nice enough guy, plenty smart and a critical thinker. But he lacks a little confidence and that gets worn like a badge on his shirt for all to see."

"Better than some of those Jr. officers with all the schooling and no practical tactical training in the field. And if they're not smart enough to know that even though they're ranked, they better listen to their Chief first or ask for suggestions, the whole Team loses otherwise."

"I agree with you there."

Andy was glad he'd recommended Sven and Kelly to Peterson. Now he was thinking he should have recommended a couple more.

As the pink glow of sunrise began to develop, the green plain ushered in some beautiful scenery, especially when they passed by small lakes that peppered the area. They encountered gazelles and several massive flocks of pelican-like birds that did more of a waterski landing on those bodies of water, wings flapping and causing quite a splash. Large white clouds rose in the pinkish-blue sky of morning.

At last, they approached several villages in a row, as the road became wider and more littered with donkey-driven carts or small lorries. Occasionally a covered troop transport passed them. Every one of the men who were awake studied those very carefully and it appeared all of them were empty—a good sign there weren't troop movements on the rise.

Traffic increased to a steady stream of two-way passage until they came to a fairly large city. None of the buildings were over three stories tall, mostly patched with layers of corrugated metal and cement material. The ground floors of most the buildings were open-air shops with vendors like one giant flea market. Now they saw scooters passing them, one with a young boy clutching a small goat behind an older man, perhaps his father.

Brightly painted schools with no doors or windows were buzzing with children beginning to congregate on the grounds. Young boys kicked around a rag-covered makeshift soccer ball. Several women and girls appeared in headdress, reminding Andy that half the population was Muslim.

Peterson had said they wouldn't be stopping along the way so they could get across the border to Benin quickly and to their proposed compound without interference and without attracting too much notice. But Andy knew hundreds of pairs of eyes had seen them—they all knew the Americans were here because they certainly weren't Chinese, and Russians used their own drivers. But Andy agreed, it was a good idea to get to their base as soon as they could.

He rifled through his pack and dug out a granola bar and a bottle of water, letting the bouncing bus lull him into being a tourist for a bit more. His stomach liked the nourishment. His eyes found the people and the colorful images fascinating.

They arrived at a checkpoint guarding the border. It was well-fortified on both sides so at each gate young men no older than high school age in the US, with semi-automatic rifles walked up and down the length of the bus and the truck ahead of them with Peterson, peering into the windows and grilling the driver with questions. He showed a sheaf of papers, which were carefully checked.

Andy made sure he didn't make eye contact with any of the border patrol. Random hot spots were common, but the fact that there were twenty of them made for more interesting scrutiny and was less likely to cause a fight. Again, he realized they'd been seen. Eyes observed and tongues would be wagging.

As they made it through the Benin checkpoint, he was struck by the number of uniformed children walking to school. The couple of towns they passed through looked slightly more prosperous. Signs in French were everywhere, unlike Niger. There were more shops, more little open-air eating places where barbeque was made over firepits made of oil barrels to rings of stone. Women and young girls wrapped themselves in colorful fabric. Several taller buildings had been built in the downtown area of one of the towns, the largest with bars on the outside Andy took for a local jail.

Just outside of the town of Kandi they entered a complex of small cottages and one large central building looking like an old school dormitory, just past a rural cemetery on a slight upslope. Outside, the perimeter was fenced in concrete and boulders, the gate made of corrugated metal, which was manually opened when they approached.

"Home sweet home, I guess," mumbled Dallas.

It had all the elements Andy was hoping for. The windows had glass. The top of the dorm building was littered with several air conditioners, past and present victims of the African heat. Three of them looked like recent installations, so he realized they'd have relief of some sort. The perimeter had a defensible wall. But better still was the fact that the complex was atop a slight swale, and anyone's approach, if by road anyway, could be easily followed.

As a base camp, Andy had to admit it was one of the best he'd seen. For his fourth deployment to this part of the world, it could have been a lot worse.

The men were housed in the common area, on cots. Private rooms with doors were relegated to their equipment and other things that needed to be guarded twenty-four hours a day on rotation. Andy was happy with this. Afterall, he was more concerned about losing their electronics and ammunition than privacy. As long as they could set up a triage room, quietly, as Peterson had instructed, where some of his medical supplies could be stored in locked storage closets, they had a fighting chance of survival even if the worst were to happen.

It was always good to look out for the worst and not to get too complacent or bored when it didn't show up. Because that's when it always did. Nothing could shoot a .50 Cal hole in a Team's confidence than not being prepared for the totally unpreparable.

He slept in their new medical unit while Dallas watched the doorway from their bunks. The last thing

Andy thought about before he dozed off was how he now felt like that one big hot dog waiting to be covered in chili, onions and melted cheese. He could feel the bush talking back to him. Somewhere a pod of monkeys howled, and a jungle dog answered without fear.

CHAPTER 7

JASPER KORNBLUM KNOCKED on Aimee's front door right at the strike of nine o'clock, just as he'd promised. He was dressed in a white suit with a bolero tie. With his white hair, moustache and well-trimmed beard, he resembled a slim and well-built Colonel Sanders. His steel blue eyes bored into her and caused a slight involuntary shiver.

"Jasper Kornblum, at your service, Mrs. Carr." His hand shot out, bridging the gap between them.

"Nice to meet you. Come in. I'm nearly ready. Can I offer you coffee?" Aimee said as she stepped aside and widened the doorway opening.

Kornblum appeared to be in his sixties, with sharp eyes that soaked in every detail of their living room. "No coffee please, but I would take a glass of water, if I can trouble you for it." He was still scanning the artwork on the walls and the detail on their unconventional stairway railing as he spoke.

Aimee fetched him a juice glass of filtered water from the counter and retreated to the bedroom to finish fixing her hair. She wore it twisted up in a swirled braid, something she hoped would keep her cooler for the hour-long drive to Sarasota.

She grabbed her shoulder bag and joined him in the living room. He pointed to the beach.

"That was the perfect spot for a wedding, and what a beautiful evening for it. Christmas Eve."

The comment warmed Aimee's heart. "Thank you. We thought so. Wanted to make it memorable for everyone."

"I regret not meeting your parents."

That familiar tug at her heart appeared and just as suddenly obeyed her internal command to disappear. "They're both gone. Would have been hard to meet them." She said it with a straight face, and it caused the older attorney to furrow his brow.

"I'm sorry. I thought that was Andy's parents."

"No, they were there." She hoisted her shoulder bag and took the water glass from Kornblum. "Shall we go?"

As they sped down the two-lane boulevard toward the freeway entrance, she felt like softening her earlier frostiness at the mention of her deceased parents.

"I want to thank you for the beautiful bowl, Mr. Kornblum. Really a lovely cut crystal pattern. Sends rainbows all over the room during the day."

"Good light. That house always had good light."

"So, you saw it before, when Mrs. Hernandez lived there?"

"Miss Hernandez, dear. She never married."

"But I thought she lived there with someone who left it for her as a life estate."

"That's true. But they never married."

"Who was he?"

"Hank Borges. Famous science fiction writer. My understanding is that they were both very happy there, eventually. I only met him once."

"Is he any good?" she asked. "I've ordered a couple of his old paperbacks."

"That's all you can find now, old, used paperbacks. I understand they are a collector's item now."

"Then I must have gotten a good deal. I think I paid thirty cents for one of them."

Kornblum chuckled. "Well, I've been misinformed. I stand corrected, Mrs. Carr."

"You can call me Aimee, please."

"And you can call me Jasper."

That made her wrinkle her nose.

"Or Mr. Kornblum, whatever makes you feel comfortable."

"It's just that—" Aimee stopped before could think how to finish her sentence.

"I'm so old? That what you mean? I'm probably older than your father. Or your father was."

That was it exactly, she mentally confirmed. "I try to be respectful of my elders. Just the way I was raised, Mr. Kornblum."

"I don't mind, child."

Several miles of freeway passed before the attorney began another conversation. "I've told you that Carmen is not well at all. They are telling me she may not even be conscious for our meeting. I'm afraid she's in her final days, so I don't want you to be shocked, Aimee."

"I understand." Thoughts of her mother's slow, painful passing and the guilt she felt when she finally died, haunted her. She was more familiar with the process than she'd ever wanted to be. "It's my fault I didn't think to reach out to her before. It's what I should have done."

"She was used to not having anyone around her. Not like there was a big family to be there during this stay. I think Carmen was a very private person, from what others have told me. And Hank wanted to make sure the estate protected her after he was gone. You see, he had a family, while she did not. He was afraid the family would try to claim the house as their inheritance, even though it was set out in his will as going to Miss Hernandez."

"An ex-wife, then?"

"Daughters. Two still alive. The former Mrs. Borges is gone."

"And should I be ready for a visit sometime?"

"I'd say not. I think that's been so long ago, and with their mother gone, the girls don't have any interest in fighting her old battles." He squeezed his steering wheel tightly and added, "Or so I've been told. But there is the issue of some of Hank's book titles being left to Carmen and not the family. But the bulk of his estate went to the family."

"So how long did they live there?"

"You mean the house at Sunset?"

"Yes."

"About ten. Until Hank's death."

Aimee wanted to ask but felt it was bad manners. Kornblum saved her the question.

"He died in a hospital, in case you were curious," he whispered. "It was very quick, a stroke." He followed it up with a kind smile, and then went back to focusing on the road.

It felt like he was pausing, trying to elicit questions from her and that made her quiet all of a sudden. Part of the excitement of the trip had left her and now she experienced some foreboding sadness.

"I'm glad you asked to see her. I was going to make an appointment to discuss some things about Carmen' estate anyway. We can do that now, if you like."

"What things?" Aimee asked.

"Miss Hernandez is a very wealthy woman. And she's going to be leaving a large portion of her assets to you, Aimee."

"And my husband."

"Yes, because you are married. But you found the house. You fell in love with it. You made the offer and purchased it before your marriage. She's going to return the money you paid for it to you, and then some."

"What?"

"You're going to inherit a significant fortune, Aimee. She has no one else to leave it to. There are some designated charities, of course, but the bulk of it will go to you."

"I'm flabbergasted." Aimee felt her hands shake. Her heart was pounding in her chest. She wished Andy was with her to hear all the news. "She doesn't even know me. We've never met, right?"

"I believe you're right, but I can't say for sure. She was very private, as I've said before. But she read a lot. Followed events. Even when she was moved to the hospital, she stayed current on things. She knew I was going to the wedding and she had wanted to hear all about it."

Aimee wondered why the woman had developed

such an interest in her.

"She also wrote novels, under a pen name. She wrote romance from that beach house and did quite well. Maybe even eclipsed Hank's work."

"Really? What under what name?"

"Callie Harmon."

"Oh my gosh! I have read several of her novels. She wrote some very sexy stuff. I stumbled upon them when I first moved to Florida because it was all about the area. I love her books."

"Well, that's a good thing." When Aimee didn't answer, he added, "because she's left her entire literary works rights to you, my dear."

"No way."

"I have the paperwork with me for you to review, if you like. I'm not allowed to give you the entire contents of the will, of course, but just wanted you to be prepared. And I thought you should know when you meet her."

Aimee was lost in thought. What sort of thing would she say to her now that she knew all this information? Did this woman do some sort of study on her? Or, why would she leave her estate to a complete stranger?

"You're asking yourself why," he said with a wry smile.

"Exactly. I've got to hand it to you. You're quite a

mind reader. Do you have an answer for me?"

"Only a guess."

"Which is?"

"I think she wanted to leave her money to someone who loved the house as much as she did. Someone who wouldn't want to tear it down and build a McMansion on it, like so many others do in the area. That's not a deed restriction when she sold you the property, but it is in the will, I will tell you that. Even if the house gets destroyed in a hurricane or other disaster, it has to be rebuilt to the original floorplan and footprint as a promise and condition of accepting the money."

Aimee was thinking about the magic that seemed to live in the house. Some of her friends had called her crazy, but now she understood her intuition had put her on the right track.

"She didn't want to spoil the magic. There is magic there," she whispered.

"And so you understand."

But do I? Do I really understand?

THE ASSISTED LIVING section of the Our Lady of Light residences did feel like a hospital. Aimee felt a slight shortness of breath, and in her gasping, she didn't finish sentences, and lost her train of thought. So much of her experience walking into this place reminded her of those sad days she came to be by her mother's side as she lay dying. It was the reason she avoided hospitals altogether.

Though the company running the facility tried very hard, with the use of pastel colors and soft lighting inside the rooms, it still had a familiar hospital odor that made Aimee begin to clench her teeth and squeeze her palms into fists. They were greeted by a male attendant who showed them to Carmen Hernandez' room.

She was dressed in a brightly colored flowered housecoat. Her hair was combed and her makeup was done. Even her nails were freshly painted bright red. Aimee had expected a much older woman, someone with gaunt cheeks sunken in, lips a light purple, with a face emerging from a nest of gray hair.

This woman before her had graying temples and plenty of streaks of light color, but her haircut was recent and she looked so healthy, Aimee wondered if there hadn't been some mistake. She was fully conscious and gave a wide smile to the two of them as they entered the room.

"There you are, dear!" Carmen said, clasping her hands together. That's when Aimee saw the IV attached to the back of her right hand, connected to a hanging bag of clear liquid next to the bed.

"You look wonderful today. I'm impressed," said Kornblum. "Whatever they're doing, you look twenty years younger, Carmen."

"Oh, nonsense. A little rouge and lipstick, some foundation and anyone can look more youthful. It's a trick, Jasper. You know it's a trick."

"But they said—" he began to object.

"*They* don't have anything to do with it. I have good days and bad days. Today is a good day. A special day. Aimee has come to see me at last."

"And I'm so sorry it took me so long. I feared I'd made a huge mistake by not coming sooner."

"Ah, but it is the magic. The magic of love. You know about this, don't you, Aimee?" she said with a sweet smile.

Aimee blushed. It was as if this strange woman knew exactly what her insides were screaming. She felt a real connection to her.

"The truth is, they have a special cocktail that makes me feel like your age, Aimee. And right after you leave, they'll whisk me into the shower, and get me back into my hospital gown, and deliver another bag. That one will have all the bad stuff and I'll be sick for three days, maybe a week. I'm getting very tired of it."

Aimee had been told she had Stage IV breast cancer. Unlike her mother, who wasted away and nearly lost all her hair even without any cancer drugs, Carmen Hernandez's hair was very healthy and thick.

"Come, pull up this chair and let's chat. Jasper, did

you tell her about the inheritance?"

While Aimee dragged the armchair closer, Jasper sat on the edge of the bed.

"I did indeed. Not all the details. Perhaps you'd like to do that yourself, Carmen."

Suddenly, her demeanor shifted, and she became distracted, frowning at her lap. "I'm going to be sick. Jasper, call the nurse."

While the attorney went in search of help, Carmen whispered to Aimee, "I had to speak to you in private. Forgive me." She winked.

Aimee took her outstretched hand and felt familiar coldness there. "I am so grateful for everything you've already done, Miss Hernandez. For selling me the house. It truly is a special place. I love the light and—"

"The magic? You feel the magic too?" Carmen asked, squeezing her hand.

"Something like that. Tell me what it was like."

"Well, I lived there for twenty years, a little more. Hank was only there half that time, unfortunately. But he used to call it his secret weapon. He couldn't write anywhere else after he had his first few novels published. So, he purchased the home and left it vacant when he wasn't there. The first time I walked inside, I felt the power of the magic. Good magic. It's the kind of magic that comes from the heart, Aimee. I think you feel it too."

She nodded her agreement and let the older woman continue.

"It's something that has to be protected. You must never tear it down or all the power will be gone. I've had offers, and I've turned down a lot of money to sell to a builder who would tear it down and replace it with something huge, but—"

Kornblum and a nurse rushed into the room.

"I'm going to have to ask you two to leave. She cannot tolerate this," the nurse said, quickly separating their hand-holding and checking her pulse, then her eyes and lastly, the drip on the bag at the side. "Miss Hernandez, you know you have to be careful. Your immune system is running on empty; your iron count is dangerously low, and we are preparing for that emergency iron infusion this afternoon."

"I know all that. Just give me a few more minutes," the older woman objected.

"Just a few. Five minutes max." The nurse moved to the other side of the bed, making notes on a whiteboard hanging on the wall. "You want something for the nausea?"

"No. I'm fine." She inhaled deeply, and, as if drawing strength. Aimee saw a slight green tint to her color—something the makeup failed to hide. Carmen continued, "All right then," she sighed. "Just before Hank's passing, I discovered my love of writing as well.

He was delighted. He started editing my work and encouraging me to write more and more. I'd just finished my first rough draft when he suddenly left us."

She wiped a tear from her cheek and stared down at her lap.

"I've ordered some of his books, Miss Hernandez. Now I plan on reading all of yours as well." Aimee was hoping it would cheer her up. "Mr. Kornblum told me about them on the way down here."

"Romance. You love romance?"

"I do."

"You believe in the Happily Ever After?" She said it as if it was a strange idol placed on a church mantlepiece.

"Absolutely I do."

Suddenly, Carmen grabbed Aimee's hand again. "You know what this means?" She searched Aimee's face, but Aimee wasn't sure what answer the older woman was looking for.

"Tell me," Aimee said, rubbing her thumb over the bony knuckles of Carmen's left hand.

"It means I will live forever, that's what it means. As long as someone is reading my books, I'll always be there. Hank and I will always be there, at that house at Sunset Beach. But you have to keep reading. Love stories. Forget his science fiction books, read love stories, Aimee."

"I will." She felt hot tears begin to form again at the tops of her cheekbones, and then spill over the ledge and drop onto her lap. The sadness was overwhelming. Aimee wondered if there was some form of dementia developing, perhaps an early stage and wondered which affliction would overtake her first—her cancer or the dementia. She decided to feed the illusion of a dying woman by telling her about her own experience.

"You are so right, Carmen. The house *is* magic. Something lives there that you can feel. I completely understand."

"Powered by love, Aimee. Don't forget that." The older woman's gaze was unwavering.

"Of course."

The nurse began to roll her eyes and motioned for them to head toward the doorway. "I think she's had enough."

"Oh, not nearly enough. There is never enough love," Carmen added stubbornly, still seeking Aimee's attention.

"We got the message, Carmen," said Kornblum. "Trust me, Aimee's not going to forget this. You can tell her more about the magic next time."

Carmen leaned forward and whispered to her, "Next time you see me, I'll be with Hank. I promise. I trust that you will keep us alive."

Her comment caused Aimee's spine to stiffen with

the bittersweet notion that life was finite, but that love was eternal. That was the message Carmen had been trying to tell her. Then she thought about Andy, so far away, the part about the finiteness of life striking a huge, gaping wound in her heart. More tears washed down her cheeks. Her eyes were now red and sore.

"There is more of the story. He's coming back, Aimee."

"Who?" asked Kornblum, his face wrinkled in a scowl.

"They both are. Hank and Andy. They're coming back and they'll never leave us again!"

CHAPTER 8

T HE TEAM PILED into the bus, along with their three Africacorps "handlers", which was a nicer way of saying the government spies. Peterson had briefed them on the fact that a thriving oil drilling business was being protected and was the private concern of the new President and several of his top generals. Andy suspected they were also into other concerns, namely drugs and girls.

So the SEALs were to thread the needle between the government forces aided by their Africacorp and coalition well-equipment troops and the ragtag rebel militia group that had been having their way with villages and animal poaching concerns in Benin, and parts of Nigeria, and were suspected of holding the journalists. The SEALs were only allowed to travel on designated roads in certain areas, just to make sure they didn't get a glimpse of something Uncle Sam wouldn't like that might end the partnership with the

US Special Forces.

But everyone expected to see the worst.

Andy noticed right away that the rear lavatory had been cleaned up overnight, however it still was missing a door. And just before they fired up the engine in the rusty white beast, someone noticed a tire had gone flat. It was an hour before a replacement tire could be located and they could get on their way.

The driver was going to let them off at the edge of a protected forest, a site being built with UNESCO funds for creation of a nature preserve of endangered species. The region was targeted by a recent IUCN Red List paper, calling out one particular species of blue baboon, well on its way to extinction. It was thought that the militia group also was responsible for poaching various other species as well, for transport to private zoos that illegally purchased the animals as breeding stock. Several old camps had been identified with use of drone footage. The SEALs single focus was for the rescue of the workers and not the animals.

The two Nigerian guides took the tip of the spear, slashing a wide path for the rest of the team to follow. Dallas and Andy were soon drenched in sweat as the party crossed a tall grassy savannah, heading into a dark jungle forest. They could hear the sounds of screaming and howling monkeys and baboons. The foliage was alive with tiny yellow birds and large black-winged duck-like creatures who were nesting in the trees above and frequently divebombed the group and came quite close to knocking hats off and sending men sprawling onto the jungle floor to avoid contact.

Andy was glad he'd brought a healthy supply of repellant and knew without it, he'd not get a wink of sleep.

The guides stopped, using binoculars to search the treetops ahead and consulting one another as to the best route to take. Peterson wasn't getting any respect from them, and each time their LPO asked for clarification and translation, he was completely ignored.

It was painful for Andy to watch. Dallas rolled his eyes.

"If he doesn't shut up, they're gonna gag him. I've seen it done," Dallas whispered.

Two hours into their hike, Andy took a drink of water and shared some with Dallas and Conley Brown, a medic first timer. He poured water on his shemagh and wrapped it around his neck and head, tying it under his chin. Then he replaced his Fresno State Bulldogs baseball cap securely on the wet headdress, the bill facing down his backside. His black gloves were full of stickers, but so far had managed to keep his hands from sustaining little cuts from the stubborn brush.

The group slowly moved forward while Andy mentally checked his pockets, adjusted the medic pack on his shoulders, and felt the reassuring bulge of his sidearm and KA-BAR. Conley walked beside him as they followed behind Dallas.

"You've been here three or four times, Andy?"

"Three. Well, I'm not sure I call the Canaries or Cape Verde part of the African continent. Way different terrain, but I've been along the coast, seen the villages there. The islands are rocks, old volcanos and really tough hiking. We took on a lot of ankle and knee injuries hiking those hills," he answered.

Conley nodded. His light pink baby's bottom skin was getting cut up and was slightly sunburned. Andy tried not to stare, but he didn't see that the boy had developed a beard yet. He'd heard about some Team Guys who lied about their age, and Conley looked younger than that even.

"You best get some sunscreen on those cheeks and lather up your nose. Make you look like a lifeguard and the girls will love it," Andy mumbled in the kid's direction.

"Yeah, I think I wiped it all off." He stopped, quickly pulling out a Warrior Wipe, which was a repellant and sunscreen all in one, wiping across his forehead, across his cheeks and over his nose.

"Careful of your eyes. You don't want to get any stuff in there, or—"

"Argh." Conley groaned. "God dammit. Too late. Mother*fucker.* Every time I do that, I feel like pissing my pants."

Andy just nodded and didn't make much of it.

"Sonofabitch that stuff stings."

"Yeah, but your eyeballs won't burn now. Thank the SEAL gods for that."

"Fuck that."

"Use your water. I got an irrigator we can use when we stop for tea and crackers." Andy grinned and wondered if he had bugs stuck in his teeth.

The sound of a chainsaw and the crack of a falling tree pierced the area, getting the guides excited. They pointed off to where the sound was coming, on the right and their conversation bubbling over as their pace increased.

Another sound of the chainsaw preceded the sight of a large tree falling very close to where they were walking, followed by the screeching sounds of chimps or baboons being displaced. They could hear multiple tools pounding and chopping wood, or perhaps nailing boards together. A campfire was burning, and the smell of food cooking filled Andy's nose, making him hungry.

Several minutes later, they encountered a clearing busy with nearly a dozen local villagers working shirtless in the filtered light of the hot sun. They were building small enclosures for animals, setting up fences and raising crisscrossed beams lashed together that would be covered in canvas or perhaps plastic membrane. A pile of metal corrugated material lay twisted and haphazardly stacked to the side. Several large dormitory-type structures were located on the other side of the clearing, made out of concrete and animal dung blocks, open glassless windows covered with canvas rags.

Peterson was shaking hands with a European-looking officer. Andy figured he was attached to the UN crew for security.

Out of one of the buildings walked Sven Tolar, who was washing his hands with a rag, smiling, headed right for Andy.

"So now my new friend is my enemy," he said in his clipped Norwegian accent. "Are you responsible for this posting?" He glanced at Peterson and the officer and shook Andy's glove and sticker-encrusted hand.

"Guilty as charged. Don't knock my clock out, Sven. But I have to say I'm really glad to see you."

"And I'm very glad to be alive, to be seen!"

"This here's Dallas, Conley. Peterson over there is the LPO. Who's your guy?"

"That's Gunnar Fucktard. Former circus performer."

Andy must have looked horrified.

"They building a zoo or breeding ground?" Andy asked.

"Who knows? They're protecting the blue baboons here. It's a humanitarian mission. They're supposed to be beautiful creatures, near extinct. This place is supposed to be a research center, someday a tourist destination, so they say."

Peterson joined them. "You must be Sven Tolar," he said, extending his hand.

"At your service, Chief."

"You get here today?" he asked.

"Yesterday. I came in with some supplies and reinforcements and a cook, but we got to travel by truck. How come you guys hiked in? There's a road just a half click away."

Peterson shrugged.

"See, they're messing with you, Peterson. They've been watching you the whole time," whispered Sven so others wouldn't hear.

"And that's why Andy here recommended you."

Gunnar began shouting orders to the Team to unpack their loads in one of the two block buildings.

"Chief, don't let him do that. He works for you, not the other way around."

"My men are tired. I'll dance with him later. Right now, I want to check in with the Headshed and let the guys rest up."

"Have you heard anything about the journalists, Sven?" asked Andy. Dallas and Conley eagerly listened for an answer.

"Some of the crew I came in with said they saw some strangers in town—there's a small town, called Benot, with a school and some government buildings and shops, a jail and an Africacorps detachment about twenty minutes away by truck. But they could have been hired workers brought in to work on the dam. They've been seeing a lot of that lately. So not sure. But they weren't from here, that's for sure."

"State's sending a bird overhead tonight. Any armed groups other than the Africacorps?" asked Peterson.

"Not yet. Gunnar and I are not quite talking that friendly yet. He's going to try to put your guys to work building latrines and finishing the pens and tree clearing, since your salaries don't come out of his expenses."

Peterson followed the men inside the dorms. Sven pulled Andy aside. "How's Kyle, and how's Tucker? He get that lady of his knocked up again?"

"Kyle's great. Aimee and I got married."

"I heard. Congrats. You sure about this?"

"Best thing I've done so far."

"She's a nice girl. You still working on that house?"

"Of course. Kind of a money pit. But she's in love

with that place." Andy continued, "Team 3 went on a training so the guys who were going to come, Kyle included, didn't make it. I thought perhaps you'd be with them."

"I took a little tour of my own up to see Kelly in Portland. I've been gone nearly a month before I came here."

"And?" Andy was hoping Sven and Kelly had rekindled their little affair they'd started during the last mission to the Canaries.

Dallas and Conley broke away and headed for the building.

"She turned me down, Andy," Sven whispered. Andy stopped in his tracks.

"Why would she go do something stupid like that? You guys were perfect for each other."

"I think Jenna's long recovery has had a lot to do with it. I keep thinking she'll be back, but she doesn't want that life now."

Andy didn't have to ask if Sven was ready for the same. At some point in his career, he knew that risking it all, leaving Aimee behind, perhaps with kids too, might not be his priority in the future. It was something every SEAL had to deal with at the end of the last mission. Kyle had told him about guys who came to talk to him, and he told Andy he could almost see that spear lodged in their chest—the blade engraved with the words: I quit. The biggest problem with quitting was facing the fear off what would come next. Would they ever find something else that excited them so, working with brothers who would die for each other?

"She's still young. Maybe she'll come to her senses," he said, placing a hand on Sven's shoulder.

"She's kinda getting used to her father-in-law's good wine and comfortable digs. And she deserves it, Andy. She'll get bored in time. And she's working with Jenna, who is still traumatized. I think she wants to help Colin with his new venture too, the security company. The one Tucker's thinking about."

"Tucker isn't ready yet." Andy was certain of this.

"I told Kyle they should send Tucker over with me. Not sure what happened. Your Peterson is going to need help, Andy. You know that, right?"

"Tell me about it."

"Even before I left Coronado to visit the Rileys, there was talk about this team being a real fuckup. Now why would Kyle put you here with these guys?"

"Because I wanted to stay in Little Creek, closer to Aimee. They lost their senior medic and Kyle thought it would be big shoes to fit into and would help me advance up the ladder."

Sven let his lower lip peel forward and shook his head, a scowl forming. "Watch yourself. Peterson is no Lansdowne. Kyle runs a pretty tight crew. Even the wives are tight, like sisters."

"Yup. That's the way it's done."

"You guys have had a run of bad luck." Sven squinted, then tapped Andy in the middle of his chest, thinking as he did so. "Nah. I think once you guys get your sea legs, you'll be fine. What you frogs need is a couple of good firefights and you'll be right as rain, you'll be communicating without saying a word, like Team 6. You'll be finishing each other's sentences before long. You'll get there," he said as he winked.

"Good to hear you say that, Sven. All the same, I'm fuckin' glad you're here."

"Shoot. I wouldn't miss this for anything. They actually *pay* me to have this kind of fun."

They both laughed.

Sven added, "What a life, right? I'm sure as hell no carpenter and they better not put me on fence detail."

"And I'm not going to go training baboons who can tear my arms out of my sockets. I don't care how endangered they are."

"Hell, I'll help them become even more endangered if they touch one hair on your head," Sven chuckled.

Andy felt like some of his jitters were floating away, just by trash talking with a man who had faced years more wartime challenges and close calls than anyone else he knew. For a while this morning and yesterday, he'd felt like he and Dallas were the only two seniors on the crew.

Which didn't bode well for a good outcome.

But with Sven by his side, at least they had a fighting chance to come out in one piece. Aimee had called it magic, the magic of their love story, and thought it would keep him safe. What it really was, Andy thought, was courage to bust through anything coming after him, and to never give up. There would be lots of blood and dust.

He wanted to walk through his front door back at Sunset Beach on his own two feet, not delivered in a pine box.

No pixie dust anywhere.

CHAPTER 9

AIMEE'S INSIDES WERE jumbled all the way home. Mr. Kornblum was smart enough to leave her alone. She'd been worried she'd say something to him she'd regret later on. Her foul mood continued, aggravated by late afternoon traffic. A downpour descended upon the car as they sped down the freeway. The bridge over to the Gulf was gleaming in the fresh rain like a giant silver arch. The sun was so bright, even through all the rain, that it hurt her eyes.

Kornblum flipped her visor down and that did give some relief.

As they traveled to the bottom of the arch, the car slowed to make the right-hand turn to Gulf Boulevard. Here the traffic was just as crowded, but only single lane in each direction, and at a considerably slower speed. He successfully dodged pedestrians who were either crossing the road to view the sunset or coming home from a day on the sand.

The attorney cleared his throat. "Can I offer you a drink, or perhaps I can treat you to an early dinner? Not sure about you, but that hospital sandwich we had for lunch wasn't all that satisfying."

"I should be the one taking you to dinner. You did all the driving. I'm not being a very good guest."

"I don't mind, dearie. You have a lot to take in. And you're facing it all on your own, with Andy being overseas." He let that sink in a bit, and then added, "How long will he be gone again?"

"This one has no set time limit. Could be a few weeks, or up to four months. We just never know." Aimee knew it wasn't the time or distance away from Andy that worried her. It was the fact that it was a new team, and Andy had said he had to find his place. He'd also confided in her that Africa continued to be one of the most dangerous places to be deployed. But she couldn't share any of that, and maybe that's what had her tangled up in the hammock of the rotten mood. "I say the dinner's on me. You pick the place, though. Pick what you want. I'm not sure how hungry I'll be."

"Very well. Seafood? Crab?"

She nodded, and then blushed at the memory of some of their early dinners out, after their love affair had flamed to perfection, the hot steamy nights, butter and crab all over her body and the effects of her margarita sparking her libido. Whatever the day's concerns were, Andy could always work it out of her, leaving her feeling soft, pliable and well-loved. She missed his tenderness. Right now, the world was looking like it was going to smack her in the eye and laugh at her cruelly.

He was pulling into Crabby Bill's and the usual scene, no matter if it was Tuesday or Saturday night. There were the early diners who came to meet their retired friends, Snowbirds, from up north, taking advantage of the specials and driving themselves carefully home in their golf carts. Later would come the younger couples and some families, who would play darts, or listen to the guitar player singing for tips and beer. And then the party scene started in earnest around eight, groups of couples or single men and women standing across the room from each other, judging the pickings or dancing to the music of a western combo.

If he'd have given her the space, she would have apologized, and given some excuse for the way she was reacting, but she couldn't think of the words to say.

What am I feeling?

But as they were shown to a table outside on the shell-strewn patio, in a corner near the parking lot, Aimee realized the noise of the early evening would probably preclude any discussions they were to have. She was okay with it.

Force of habit with a touch of melancholy allowed her the space to order her favorite strawberry margarita. Kornblum ordered a beer.

"Well, Aimee, I'd say we were pretty lucky. Carmen was having one of her good days. I'd say, the best I've seen her."

"I was expecting someone way more infirmed, especially for someone under hospice care. I've seen people walking around all over the place who look dead compared to her. She's very sharp. At least she was, until the end when she was talking about Hank coming back to her. Doesn't it usually work that she would go join him? And she mentioned Andy—"

"It happens at this stage, Aimee. I had a long conversation with her on the phone one day. I actually think she forgot who I was. Perhaps might have mistaken me for Hank. She was prattling on about everything she'd done that day, and of course none of it was true. She doesn't drive any longer. She certainly doesn't go swimming in the ocean any longer."

"But she used to."

"Yup. She's very convincing, so it's hard to really know where she's coming from. She's describing the place she's traveling to. Like another one of her adventures. They used to meet up over the years before they lived together. And then she'd go back to California and he'd return to New York. Boy would I like to be a fly on the wall in those days." He smiled into his glass and took a long swig of his beer.

"I've had a little experience with my parent's estate when they passed. And it was important that we documented everything while my mother was well enough to be considered of sound mind. Don't you worry about that with Carmen?"

"I think she knows what she's doing. We've kept our business meetings very short, and I only proceed when I'm certain all the marbles are in place. I also usually get a witness to everything she signs, someone who isn't on my payroll. And I've never been asked to do anything that I felt was bad for her, or for someone else. It is her desire that you inherit her money, Aimee. She could give it all away to charity, but she wants you to use it. To have it to enjoy."

"As long as the house remains the same size."

"That's a requirement. You can modernize it, but you can't tear it down. And if it's damaged in a hurricane, and it has been damaged over the years, it has to be rebuilt to the same size it is now."

"I think I understand better what she meant by doing that. Almost like the house captured, trapped something there that will escape if it's torn down." She sipped her drink, closed her eyes and pretended Andy was home, sitting right in front of her. But of course, he wasn't there when she opened her eyes.

"I set it up today so you can go back on your own and visit, if you like."

Aimee was touched with his gesture. "Why is she doing all of this? Has she told you? Why me?"

"Because you loved the house in its dilapidated condition and have now restored her to the beauty it was when she lived there. When they lived there. In a way, she's put you on a mission—a mission to explore inside yourself what the house brings out of you. Almost as if it's an old friend and not just a physical house at all. She's treating it like a sentient being, in a way."

"Do you know the history of the property? Is there something else I'm not aware of? Some backstory?"

He shrugged. "You'd have to ask her. All I know is that they were very happy there. It was his touchstone, a place where his creative energy could expand, where he could write his books. I'm guessing she wants the same for you. She found her writing ability there. Maybe you have some talent you haven't explored yet. Who knows?"

On the way home, Kornblum surprised her with his comment.

"You haven't asked me how much money is in her estate, Aimee. Aren't you curious?"

"I don't want to know." It was out before she could retract it. "Neither one of us came from real money. I have to honestly say I've never chased it, either."

He gave a belly laugh. "Boy, young lady, I don't run across many people like you. It's usually the first thing anyone asks."

"I just want to know why."

He walked her to the front door and extended his hand. "Nice to spend some time with you today, Aimee. I hope you get all your questions answered, and if I can help in any way, just give me a ring."

"Thanks, I will. You've been very generous with your time."

"I still work for Carmen. She asked me to prepare you and was delighted when you wanted to meet her. I hope that when the time comes, I can help you manage your estate as well, but that's entirely up to you. So, you see, there is a bit of a selfish motive there. I am an attorney, after all."

She laughed, feeling comfortable around him. "Well, we've made a good start then. Thanks again."

Aimee watched him pull out from the driveway, back up, and then wave to her as he exited to find the road back to Tampa. She dialed her front door code and took a step across the threshold but stumbled on something at her feet. She found a small brown box, so small, in fact, that she'd missed it entirely when she started inside. The box was tied with a piece of white ribbon about a quarter inch wide, ending in a bow.

Aimee shook the box and it rattled. She examined the underside and all the edges to see if there was a note or some sort of notation written anywhere indicating where it had come from. She turned around and searched the alleyway and didn't find any curious onlookers. When she untied the ribbon, she found a small bracelet made from objects she'd seen on the beach over the past year she'd lived there.

There were several shells, mostly white, but many with colors of yellow, purple and rose and where a hole had developed along its journey to her hands, someone had used a piece of wire and twisted it carefully to attach the shells to the bracelet. There was a smooth turquoise piece of sea glass, with wire crisscrossing and encapsulating it, and then attaching it to the rest of the strand. There was a pink piece of lacey calcified coral, a smooth black pebble and a yellow and clear cat's eye marble, all with tiny holes inserted in them so that they could be attached to the rest of the strand. As she examined the objects, she also found a partial bottle cap, and an orange plastic fish charm, as well as a green plastic coffee cup stopper.

Someone had installed a clasp between two charms and when Aimee opened it up and placed the bracelet around her wrist, it fit perfectly. She snapped it closed and held her hand out in front of her, shaking the little pieces so lovingly stitched together.

On her heel, she whirled around to face the alleyway again.

"Is anyone out there?" she called, her voice echoing against the concrete carport pad and bouncing against the walls of the place next door. "Hello? Did you make this for me?"

Listening for any sign of life, she walked out to the alleyway and first looked to her right, and then her left.

"I'd like to say thank you. It's very beautiful," her voice echoed to the silent houses and cars nearby. "Very unusual, and everything looks like you found them here on this beach, which makes it even more special. Won't you come out and talk to me? I'd like to personally thank you for it."

But no one answered.

On her steps back to her still-opened front door, she examined the box inside to determine if there had been any clue left as to who either the artist or the giver was. But just like the silent alleyway, she found no clue as to who had left this gift for her.

One last time she studied the garage and alleyway from her porch. "Thank you. It's beautiful. I'll take good care of it."

Aimee set the box on the coffee table, kicked off her shoes and was on her way to the kitchen for some water when something caught her eye. Through the living room sliding glass door, she saw where someone had drawn a heart in the sand. Inside were two names:

Aimee and Andy.

When she saw how her name was spelled, using the proper spelling her mother had given her, not a more common way to spell Aimee, she knew all of a sudden who had made this bracelet for her, meant as a wedding present.

Logan!

She scanned the beach in both directions as the orange glow of sunset covered everyone and the stiff peaks of purple clouds slowly bloomed in the sky. It was impossible to see everyone's faces, but no one looked in her direction. Retrieving her cell from her jacket pocket, she took a quick picture of the heart and their names drawn on her patio.

Aimee ran to their bedroom and pulled out two of Andy's long-sleeved work shirts she'd hung up from the dryer and didn't need ironing. She folded them into a small square, one on top of the other, then added a pair of his jeans, rejecting Andy's paint jeans and opting for a decent pair with no holes in them. She got out an old pair of running shoes he'd recently complained about, and two pairs of thick socks, two pairs of briefs and two white V-necked T-shirts. She also found a light-weight jacket that would make a good windbreaker and could be worn in warm weather. She removed a small tube of toothpaste and a toothbrush she'd gotten from her dentist at her last cleaning, still wrapped in plastic.

Everything was neatly folded and placed in one of her shopping bags. She added a bar of soap, and some liquid hand sanitizer, two apples, two bananas and a half loaf of wheat bread. She also found a small unopened mango juice container, and two water bottles.

The bag was heavy as Aimee lifted it to her door and set it down on the doormat. To the empty carport and alleyway beyond, she shouted, "Thank you. Please accept these as my appreciation. I will leave more food tomorrow, if you like this. Please stay safe and warm, Logan." Her voice faltered as her eyes filled with tears. "Just remember that I love you. That mom and dad always loved you until their last day. Let me help you, Logan. Let *me* be *your* big sister for a change. I want to help."

Everything was still eerily quiet, but she felt someone was watching her all the same. Andy's words, and those of the doctor she'd spoken to at the hospital where Logan had been in detox came shouting out to her.

Be careful. He could be dangerous. Don't do anything stupid. He may not be the big brother you once knew.

And Andy had made her promise she'd do that, made her promise she'd not try to contact him or go looking for him while he was gone. But that was before Logan reached out from the near dead of the streets and touched her heart by making something with his own hands. And he also showed her that perhaps he knew about the wedding, for how else could it explain the heart drawing in the sand?

This means there is hope. This means a part of him I've loved all those years still remain.

Aimee left the bag on the mat, closed her front door and locked it. She wasn't stupid. Of course, she should lock all her doors and windows and take every precaution available to her. She also had another idea. She called her teacher friend, Shelley.

"How *was* the meeting, Aimee? And have you heard from Andy yet since he's been gone?" She was always direct and didn't sugarcoat anything.

"Not since he got there. I might hear tonight. But, Shelley, after I got home seeing Carmen Hernandez, I got a beautiful package left for me on my doorstep. It's a bracelet, made from found things at the beach. Shells, a bottle cap, a marble, pieces of coral. It's really beautiful, and a little crude, but he made it with his own hands."

"Who made it?"

"Logan. I know it was Logan."

"Oh dear, did you see him lurking around your door or something?"

"No. And that's a little unkind, don't you think?"

"Well, he does have a drug and alcohol problem. You don't want to mess around with that, Aimee. I thought Andy made you promise—"

"Yes, he did. But I'm being careful."

"You still keep the gun beside your bed?"

"Yup, in the bedside table. Just like when I was living in the bungalow last summer. But Shelley, I think this is a really good sign. I think it was a call for help."

"You're not qualified. He needs professional help."

"But he's my brother. He reached out to me. Am I supposed to just turn my back on him?"

"You're not turning your back on him. You're getting him the help he needs. He doesn't need a friend who likes his jewelry. He has much larger issues. You don't know how sick he is, and I'm pretty sure Andy would be upset if he thought you were trying to encourage him."

Aimee wiped the thought out of her mind, refusing to listen to that little voice of doubt coming from the back of her head. "You should see the bracelet. It's so unusual."

Shelley's voice became quiet. Then she asked the question Aimee didn't want to answer. "So, what did you do, Aimee?" Shelley knew her all too well.

"I gave him some clothes. Well, I didn't see him, of course. But I gave him a couple pairs of Andy's old jeans, still in good shape. A couple shirts, some under-wear, a pair of running shoes, and toiletries—soap and toothpaste."

"Unbelievable," Shelley sighed into the phone.

"I've locked all my doors and windows. Just to be sure."

"Um hum." Shelley was unusually quiet while Aimee also told her about the bananas, waters and the mango juice and hand sanitizer.

"I just wanted to help, that's all. Wouldn't you do the same? What if it was one of your kids, living on the street? Wouldn't you do something?"

"I'd call the cops."

"No, you wouldn't. I know you, Shelley. You're just as kind-hearted as I am."

"There's a reason they tell you not to give the peo-ple at the grocery store money. They buy drugs and alcohol with it."

"I didn't give him any money."

"Oh. My. God. I should hope not."

"I gave him clothes and stuff that would be good for him."

"You know you're wasting your time justifying what you did."

Aimee felt her anger brewing and didn't appreciate Shelley's lack of compassion.

"You're a fucking snob, Shelley." She immediately

regretted the outburst.

"Oh yeah? So, answer me this one question, Aimee. Why did you call me? Why even check the windows and doors? You know you were acting a little reckless. What would happen if he knocked on your door? If he showed up on your patio?"

"Well, he already did that."

"Oh, Jesus. I can't believe I'm hearing this. Now I'm going to call the cops."

"No, it wasn't like that. He made a drawing in the sand. A heart. Inside, it had both our names in it. He was telling me he knew about the wedding. Shelley, this gives me hope. Hope that my brother, whatever faults he has and no matter what health issues are going on with him, that there's some part of him—a good, healthy part of him that remains. I want to appeal to that good side, that healthy part of him, not treat him like a criminal or street urchin. I think you're heartless, Shelley."

Aimee could hear her heavy breathing and knew she was biting her tongue.

"And I'm sorry about the part about you being a snob. That was unkind of me."

In a very measured voice, Shelley revealed her thoughts. "Aimee, this isn't Disneyland, my friend. You have to start living in the real world, not the one you want it to be. Let the people who are professionals do their job. You need to get out of the way, even if you think you're being cruel."

"But—"

"Just imagine this. What would happen to him if he caused you harm? What if you encouraged him too soon, made a judgment about what he was thinking and who he was, when in actuality that didn't begin to describe who he's become, Aimee? And, if he really wanted to gain access to your house, wouldn't he have a pretty easy time breaking your sliding glass door down? He could do it with a lawn chair, or one of your bricks on the patio. Are you telling me you'd shoot him? Or, would you hesitate?"

"I think you're making more out of this than needs to be."

"So, ask yourself honestly the answers to those questions. And the real reason you called me? You wanted to feel safe. You'd better check your gut, Aimee. And, I think you should come over and stay with me tonight, and then let's go call Social Services or that doctor you met with and ask them what to do. Because, if you think you can help him on your own, you might make everything worse."

CHAPTER 10

FIRST LIGHT OF day, Andy requested he be able to call Aimee on his cell. Peterson asked him to wait until they had a day in the city of Benot, which had been planned for tomorrow.

"Not worried about the technology of a group finding you as I am your bubble showing up in someone's internet preferences here, and then that information gets relayed to someone else who can cause us a problem. And I'm the only one authorized to use the SAT phone," Peterson said.

Andy could see it was hard for him to tell him no.

"So, am I on the team doing some reconnaissance in the jungle, or working the equipment?"

"Did you get your triage set up?"

"All done, sir. Your new man, Conley Brown. He's got a good head on his shoulder. He organizes like it's *DIY Benin Jungle, Season 4*. I can tell they've put those guys through some still drills to have them work that fast. I don't remember being taught that."

"He's been around it all his life. His mother is a Navy doc, stationed right now in Djibouti."

"No shit?"

"That's what I'm told. He's serious about not being a *One and Done*. Plans to get his twenty in."

"He's a good candidate for it," agreed Andy. "So, you didn't answer my question."

"Well, if you're not needed with the setup, then sure, I'd like you and Sven to take several guys and head south to a plain, a small savannah atop Mont Sokbaro. It's a day trip. You'll be on your own overnight, come back tomorrow morning. We got drone footage of some local trails. We need to check on something that showed up."

"You're gonna want it painted?"

"Only if you identify something. I'll give you the com so we can do a three-way with our friendlies in the sky. What our bird can see, so can others. I don't need them to know we're looking there, if you get my drift."

"Understood."

"You want me to pick the team?"

"Yessir. I'm not quite up to date on the skillset."

"Head back to the bunker and get Sven packing. I'll meet you there with my list, and I'll send others I see over there. Make sure Conley knows he's not to be giving Viagra to the locals, okay? And no animal medicine in our surgery, got it?"

"Fuck no. You think—"

"Gunnar Larssen is a bullshitter from way back. We gotta work with him, but if I catch anything dirty on him, I'm reporting it. He has a huge authority complex. He's going to be envious of some of your equipment, particularly the disinfectants and antibiotics and pain killers. All the expensive stuff."

"Must be something in the water, sir."

"I'm not tracking, Andy."

"Seems like everyone is trying to seize power, using other resources to get it, or get one over on everyone else."

"We're talking centuries of uprisings and violence. They squander their freedoms fighting for everything. No one is strong enough to overcome it. So, Uncle Sam, the Chinese, Russians, we all add our powder to the mix and wham! Someone gets power who shouldn't have. One thing's for certain, it isn't about the blue baboons, or the people or even about the ecosphere. It's all about power and who has it, and who doesn't."

Andy didn't have much to say, except to internally notice Peterson actually understood a lot more about the dynamics of Western Africa than he let on. It was running a Team he was light on. He wasn't sure if that was a good thing or not.

"Sir, can I recommend someone to you?"

"Go ahead. I got turned down for several I said were critical. Who?"

"You need Tucker Hudson. You need Fredo, Danny Begay, and his cousin who is a SWCC boat guy, if we'll be doing anything on the Niger River. Armando and T.J. would be good too. But Tucker. He's the key. He's like the glue. Second time around for him and the man is tough. Sven is great, but he's not American-grown, and that makes a difference. The men trust Tucker. And, you need a couple of bullies standing up or silencing Mr. Larssen. Fredo has a way of using humor to knock a guy off his perch. Is Gunnar even military any longer?"

"Supposed to be strictly on the UN payroll. But we don't know who else has him by the balls. I'm really not happy to have to work with him, and I've only been here not even a day."

Peterson drew a line in the red dusty soil. "Tucker's expecting a little one any day, Kyle told me. And he doesn't want to miss the birth. You know how that is. It's not his time up, so for a special duty, he's got to be willing."

"That's too bad. How much longer?"

"He didn't tell me. I think soon. But this is baby #2, so anything goes. You know that."

"Indeed, I do."

"Well, maybe Brandy and the kid will cooperate, and he can get out of night feedings and come join the circus over here, sir."

"Wouldn't that be something?"

Several minutes later Andy and Sven were trading equipment and admiring their packs. It was a common thing to do, show customization for little compartments used to stash their tools of choice. Like tattoos, showing off their gear or some cool feature they'd stitched into their bags—toolbelts to protect and hold that gear, was a pastime. Almost like a pissing contest and it helped spend hours of waiting or non-sleep when they were just too wired.

Dallas' shadow completely filled the doorway. Behind him, stood Archie Nolan, Kit Holmes, Connor Lannahan and Qwanme Jones. Jones was the only one bigger and taller than Dallas, having just taken leave of a lucrative football career to join up with the Teams after his little brother was killed in Afghanistan some five years prior. Andy made the introductions to Sven, getting help from the team filling in the blanks.

Peterson arrived last.

"Dallas, you're point man on this, and I want you right next to him, Sven. We got four of you who speak French, which will have to do. Benin has some fifty dialects and ethnic languages, and we'd not be ready until the next century if we had to be fluent in any of them."

The team grumbled agreement.

"Last night we got some good drone footage of a nice grassy area—" he pulled out a map of West Africa, pointing to a northern central region of Benin. "This here is Mont Sokbaro, and it's a favorite for excursions to capture baboons, chimps and some Western African Gorillas, mostly for poaching breeders for zoos, since it's a big no-no to capture underage or females with little ones. They identified a couple sites here and here." Peterson showed two lighted areas taken with night vision photography. "You need to check out both camps, determine if they're civilian or militia, or *otherwise*. They have the advantage of heavy tree coverage, so a night drop was deemed unfeasible. But they can't hide everything."

Off to the side of both areas were perimeter square-shaped probably stone and block structures, and inside the heat signature showed a dotting of humans, either troops overnighting or setting camp, or kidnap victims.

"Quite common here is the kidnapping of school-age children for ransom. But aid workers? Those are greatly prized." Peterson said and set his jaw, grinding his teeth. "One thing you don't see are vehicles. No roads here. Lots of rough turf, even though the mountain forms a nice plateau, it's still too rough for an airstrip. So, figure everyone who's here has hiked up, same as you. And if there are prisoners or children, you have to figure they would have suffered under the laborious journey."

The men passed around the IR black and white photos, occasionally pointing to mountain trails or other items of interest.

Sven had a question. "So other than the guys left back at base, who are our backups?"

"We're to call State first, then the Africacorps. They earn a decent wage here, and come from all over Central Africa, but they can easily be hired by the militias, who pay a lot better. And, of course, they'll be more motivated to fight to save their own farms and communities. When those guys desert, they take their guns and equipment and maps with them."

One of the men asked if anyone had taken direct responsibility for the aid workers abduction.

Sven was quick to answer. "New groups sprouting up all the time. These aid workers are like cash cows to them. They are easy targets, usually have family somewhere who care about them and can pay up. Even the municipal police are sometimes in on it, or try to take over someone else's operation."

"And from what the Headshed told me, the Africacorps guys go home whenever violence starts erupting back at home, unless they're conscripted criminals. They'll work for the highest bidder, so don't count on them." Sven was all program now, not an ounce of frivolity in his tone of voice.

Andy asked the crowd if anyone had more questions or had noted something they hadn't noticed. The room was silent.

"These guys aren't evil, the ones who cause all this mayhem. They're opportunity players and generally not well trained. But some of them have served along some of our Special Forces, and they notice everything. Do not show photographs, maps, or do anything to make them think we're a forward guard of some small invasion or rescue army. They switch sides frequently, depending on who is paying. They'd prefer peace, but war is way more profitable. After generations in a row now of destabilizing wars, most of them have not known what peace even looks like."

Andy added, "And you're not going to win their hearts and minds by being a nice guy. They play rough, and hard and they are constantly looking for opportunity to remove certain things from your possession. So we should stay in twos. No lone wolf forays into the bush. You're liable not to come back."

Peterson handed Jones the com and watched as it was slipped into a padded pocket on the footballer's backpack. He handed Dallas and Andy each a SAT phone. Sven didn't attempt to hide his disapproval that he didn't get one. Qwanme passed out Invisios to everyone. They tested batteries on everything they brought, and then announced the party's departure in thirty minutes.

The jungle gave some relief from the scalding sun, except for small clearings which sometimes were just naturally dried-up finger lakes, or places where a building or residence had once resided. As they began to climb at the base of the four-hundred foot "hill" that shouldn't have been called Mont anything, Andy turned around to look at where they'd been. The sweeping vistas here were unlike anything else he'd seen in Northwest Africa. Thin fingers of light smoke drifted around in spots on the valley floor carrying with it the scent of barbeque.

At a distance, the whole plain below looked like some National Geographic special on the landscape of an underpopulated land famous for shipping more slaves to England and the Eastern United States than just about anywhere else. Yet it looked so serene and peaceful.

After several grueling hours, by midafternoon, they had reached what would have been a summit if Mont Sokbaro hadn't blown its top centuries ago. What lay in the area before them was a lush, green valley over-populated with vines and twisting trees covering up the jagged edges of the crater's rim. Their feet padded across the red loamy soil easily five hundred feet deep that had at one time covered the entire area. Steam emanated from the red clay, indicating an abundance of moisture and the bio breakdown of dead branches and trees.

At an abandoned school or government building of some kind, they stopped to take refreshment, study the maps again and set up a temporary night camp.

Andy's calves were burning and his ankles were sore from little stumbles and caused him to bring all his weight down on a turned foot. It was going to feel good to stop, and maybe they'd let him have just ten minutes of meditation, before they'd prepare their evening meal. He knew the instant spaghetti was going to taste damned good. He'd even lick the damned container, he was so hungry.

CHAPTER 11

"HAVE YOU MADE the call yet?" Shelley asked.

Aimee had gotten up late, still in a rotten mood. They tried to talk when she arrived at Shelley's house last night. She probably had too much wine, and then she began the worry about what had been wafting around the back of her head now for the past twenty-four hours: no call from Andy.

She knew it was entirely unrealistic to hear from him so soon. He'd warned her of this. She'd been through it once already since they'd gotten together, but it still didn't help her courage. Shelley was a good friend, but she trusted Andy's advice, especially when it came to street smarts. He had, after all, been a great help to Corey, the SEAL she'd been dating, Andy's best friend, before Andy came out to visit and they fell in love.

Corey would be the *last* person she'd ask for advice, even though he was well familiar with drug and alcohol addiction.

She felt like she was freefalling, in limbo. Her once perfect world might still be perfect, but now the edges of that story were lightly singed. Nothing was as it appeared. Now she wondered about her trust of the attorney, Jasper Kornblum. What was she to think about the estate and inheriting money she never asked for? And why was she chosen? She still had no answer to that.

It was like a great big five-thousand-piece puzzle dumped on the table without a picture to follow. Parts of the whole thing lay scattered in front of her. Where should she start? What was the information she needed to make a correct decision? Should she contact her ladies on Andy's new team for support, people she hadn't even met, like she would have on his old Team 3? What would they think about her having a drug-addicted homeless brother? Shelley wanted her to call the police, but what if that would mean an extra layer of violence on her brother just at the time when he was trying to reach out?

"Aimee, I asked you a question," Shelley demanded. Her hardness wasn't necessary, and it rankled her.

"Shelley, would you just stop pushing me? I can't figure anything out when I'm under pressure."

"What's to figure out? You're in danger, Aimee."

That really started the fires of hell. She stood,

pointing to her best friend. "Dammit, Shelley, I said back off!"

Shelley whirled around the retreated to the kitchen where she proceeded to empty the dishwasher and bang pots and pans together, making a heroic gesture to let her know she was put out too.

Aimee didn't feel she owed an apology to anyone. It would have been the "nice" thing to do, but she just didn't feel like it. At the moment, she didn't care if Shelley thought she was being selfish, or that her bratty behavior came as the result of her feeling entitled. Shelley's own story had been ragged and a bit raw and she'd seen a much more difficult slice of life than Aimee had.

But that still was no excuse.

She peered around the corner and watched Shelley brew more coffee and wash her hands in the sink. Her friend looked up at her while drying her hands in the dishtowel, discarding it with a toss onto the counter-top. She crossed her arms and waited for an apology Aimee knew she expected, but she would not give.

"I'm going to go back home and make my calls there. I think I will be more relaxed. I know you mean well, but I can't stand you hovering over me while I do it. You're right to be concerned about me and Logan. I get that. But I can't think straight here, I just can't."

"No one's holding you against your will, Aimee.

I'm fine with you leaving any fucking time you want. And I'll probably be here the next time you call in a panic."

"I *wasn't* in a panic."

"You knew and still know you're in danger. Don't try to do this alone, Aimee. I know I've said it a dozen times by now. That's not a healthy way to do it."

"But I have to do it my way, Shelley."

"Okay, suit yourself. But if I can't get hold of you, I'm calling the cops."

It was a standoff, a compromise. And they didn't lose their friendship over it. It was as good as Aimee could get today from her best friend.

When she returned to her place, the bag with the clothes and food items was gone. Nothing was left in its place. She remembered that she'd promised to give more food next time, so she set her overnight bag down, and began making a sandwich for Logan, then added another one. Anxious to get this easy decision out of the way, she wrapped them up, added more apples and one last banana, some waters again and a couple granola bars. At the last minute she slipped in two disinfectant wipes Andy always brought with him on fishing trips and on deployment.

She set the brown lunch bag on the doormat and locked the door.

The sand message had dried, and the edges partially collapsed. She went out onto the beach on a very mild winter day without a cloud in the sky. The warm sand felt good on her bare feet and she vowed to get back into her running routine again. It did help her make decisions and sort out her concerns in life.

Maybe that's the problem.

Her cell phone pinged, and she didn't recognize the number. She scrolled for something from Andy and found none. Then she looked up her directory and called Dr. Denby at the Sunshine Palms Treatment Center.

It took nearly two minutes before Denby came on the line.

"How are you, Aimee? Anything new about your brother?"

"I'm good. We got married on Christmas Eve. Andy's on deployment, but oddly enough, I think Logan is reaching out to me."

"Really? How?"

"I think he made me a bracelet from stuff we find at the beach. Shells, rocks, pieces of wire. He left it in a box on my doorstep."

"So, he knows where you live?"

"Apparently."

"And how do you know it's Logan?"

"Well—" she wasn't going to tell him it was a hunch or that it looked like something Logan would make, but that was the truth. Then she remembered the heart drawn in the sand. "He drew a heart with both of our names in it, on my back patio, in the sand. He spelled my name correctly, Dr. Denby, which almost never happens. But I think this was a wedding present to me. I took it to mean it was a sign he was reaching out." She examined the charms hanging around her wrist. "Very carefully done. Beautiful. Like he put his heart into it."

"Well, Aimee, I have to admit we don't usually see that. Usually the kind of contact families have with their member is ransacking the home, stealing stuff, or begging for money, promising to get clean. Money for a bus ticket to a rehab place they have no intention of visiting. Very sad. But I have to warn you."

"Yes, I knew this was coming."

"Well, Logan can be very charming when he's in control. I saw a glimpse of it a time or two. But I really worry about all the damage living on the street has permanently done to his body. And these patients don't usually have an epiphany and all of a sudden get clean on their own."

"But couldn't this be the first step?"

"Possible. Anything is possible. But you have to be prepared for the opposite as well. Don't put too much faith in it. And now we have the problem of him knowing where you live. And you live alone now?"

"Yes."

"See, that's a problem. He didn't show up when your husband was around, so that's a red flag in my book, Aimee. And I have to tell you to please be very careful."

She sighed, flopping her body onto the buttery yellow leather couch, watching the waves outside. "I gave him some clothes, and a little bit of food." She expected a scolding.

"I see," Dr. Denby said calmly. "It would be harmless if you weren't so vulnerable. One thing they do, Aimee, and they do it really well, is calculate whom they can use to get what they need. They're expert at taking advantage, look for opportunities to do so. The moral code is corrupted, overpowered by years of abuse. You can't assume they think straight, or even care as much as you think they do. And they'll use that, too. Use it against you to get what they want."

"But I can afford to help him, just a little bit. I'm not giving him money. I gave him some clothes, some water bottles and fruit, sandwiches. No money. I know better than that."

"So, you're like training a wild dog or cat, trying to coax him into your world. That usually doesn't work out very well. You have to be careful, and I'd recommend not doing any of that going forward."

"But what do I do?"

"I think you need to go down to the police department and have a discussion, so they have a file on you, and on him. Just in case you call with a problem. And you should tell them that as far as you know, he's not been violent with anyone and he doesn't have a weapon, or you don't suspect he does. That's very important. How you call for help can make the difference between life or death for him. The police are charged with your safety, even at the expense of his. It's how they're trained."

"So, I should make a complaint, then?"

"It's called an incident report. You can recommend that he be given another stay here, if you like, something other than going to jail if he acts out or violates the law. He may not know any longer where his own boundaries are, or yours either."

"I feel so helpless."

"You'd be doing him a service to report it, Aimee. I think your husband would want you to do the same, especially since you're alone. And can I recommend something else?"

"What?"

"Get a dog. Get a grown dog who will be protective and will bark when someone's around."

Aimee immediately thought that would be a good idea. "Where would I go?"

"There's a no-kill shelter not far from you. I can text you the phone number. Sometimes you have to pay vet fees if they're a rescue or were abandoned. And the neuter or spay fee. It's a good way to get a friendly, watchful friend."

"They don't allow dogs on our beach, but there's a dog park nearby. I like that suggestion, doctor."

"Good. But you also should make that report, and I'd do it today. And don't leave anything else on your stoop. You have to ask yourself what if it isn't Logan, but someone using him and his identify somehow to get something from you."

"Okay, I'll do it this morning. Can I have them call you?"

"No, they won't do that. You can mention that I've treated him before, and I might get a call if they pick him up, but no guarantees. They're very busy, and if he's broken the law, I most definitely won't be called. Nor will you."

Dr. Denby also gave her the phone number of a local NAMI chapter, and encouraged her to start to attend meetings to learn about mental illness.

"You will find fellowship amongst the other families who have dealt with this heartbreaking situation. These are people you can talk to about things no other person would begin to understand. You will learn from them, Aimee. Give them a shot."

"Thank you."

After her phone call, she checked the front porch and found the brown paper bag gone.

CHAPTER 12

ANDY WAS AWAKENED by Dallas, who put his finger up to his lips, indicating to keep quiet. He couldn't figure out where he was at first. The dark night was the blackest he'd ever seen, figuring there wasn't an incandescent light within twenty miles of the camp.

But there was enough of a moon to see the silvery outlines of expressionless faces, packs, boots, cots and tall bushes tossing from side to side in the stiff African savannah breeze.

Dallas pointed to his own ear, so Andy retrieved his Invisio to be able to hear what their point man was going to whisper.

"There's a large encampment on the other side of the clearing. Sven and I took our NV goggles and the whole place lit up. I'm going to paint the corners. Give Peterson a call and let him know we have at least 60 count. We gotta get close, get some pictures and get the hell out of here tonight."

"Roger that," he whispered, and dialed.

"Holy shit. Combatants or prisoners?" Peterson demanded, as Dallas stepped into the huddle a few paces in front of Andy.

"Don't know yet. We're getting in close to give you some markers. Make sure they sent that bird up tonight."

"No, it's planned. They might already be there."

Dallas gave him the hurry-up sign. "Gotta go. We're not staying tonight, so look for us and if you hear something, that would be bad news."

"God speed. That phone has a locator. Make sure it stays on so the men upstairs will know."

"Roger that."

Dallas indicated they go single file behind him. Archie and Kit came next, their very white skin reflecting off the moon. Andy tapped Kit on the back and handed him a jar of face paint they took turns using as they followed the trail. Qwanme grinned, pushing Andy's hand away to turn down the goop, as he called it, his big white teeth reflecting in the limited light. His skin was already darker than the night sky.

Monkeys occasionally called out and were answered, as if they also had a perimeter that was guarded. With their NV goggles, eyes stared back at them from the bushes, following their progression.

Two guards were sitting on two flat rocks, slumped

over and snoring loudly, facing one another, their rifles slung across their shoulders. One had a long-sleeved hooded sweatshirt in a dark color. The other one wore some kind of soccer jersey from a team Andy didn't recognize.

A bonfire was burning a short distance away, blinding them at first, then illuminating the walls of the old school or storage building without doors or windows. Inside, they heard coughing sporadically and in one case, Andy was sure it was that of a child. Sven turned and faced him.

"Children," he whispered.

Dallas used three fingers to indicate the others were to run perimeter in the other direction and take pictures. Immediately the two of them turned and headed the opposite direction, toward the backside of the structures, flipping to IR.

"Watch out for animals."

At first, Andy wasn't sure what he meant. But all of a sudden, they heard a donkey bray not far away. They froze in place until several minutes passed to make sure it wasn't a defensive trumpeting of their position.

Dallas retrieved the tubes of paint from his pack, turned on his scanner so he could see where he poured the paint laced with iron and other metal shavings. He slowly walked along the outer wall of the building. This specialized marking would enable the drones to pick up the signal without problem. He squeezed the bottle, which looked like a catsup container, sending bits of liquid out in front nearly two feet. A clear and odorless liquid, in daylight, it wouldn't be visible without a scanner like he had tonight.

Andy followed behind, watching for signs of another sentry turning to face backwards often to check for someone following them. He snapped pictures silently, sending them to Peterson for the upload. He was trying to lean into an open window to take a picture of what looked like young children when he heard the sounds of water falling and realized he was standing not more than three feet away from a little boy peeing in the night. He completely froze and let the kid do his business.

It was all over in less than a minute. The kid, probably scared of the dark, ran back inside the large room and disappeared into the sea of bodies. Dallas returned, and they waited until it sounded like no one else had awakened, and then snapped shots of the blackness inside the open window they hoped would reveal something when properly projected.

Dallas pointed a reverse course to head back where they started, shooting everything, including boulders and felled trees.

When they met up with the other group, Kit Holmes was eager to tell them something. He got close, whispering, "Found some ammunition crates and some spent rounds, even some .50 Cal, as well as empty C4 containers lying around. Looks like they brought in a pygmy railroad car by helicopter and dropped it here. All locked up. I'm betting they're storing some serious firepower there."

"That's good intel. Somebody's been practicing."

"A training camp?" Archie asked.

Dallas shrugged. "How about you?" he asked Sven.

"I'm guessing yes. This isn't a garrison. I want to see the pictures when we get back."

"Nobody saw any evidence of our hostages, then?" Andy posed.

The collective shaking of heads was disappointing, but part of the job was eliminating possibilities.

They returned to their base, quickly retrieved everything, covering up all indication anyone was there, and quietly crept through the lip of the crater and down the side. Medium-sized rocks rolled down the sides of the hill, several men sliding on their butts when they almost took a twisted ankle fall. It took them nearly an hour to come down the sides that took only half that time on the climb.

At the bottom, they removed their sweaty helmets and stopped for a water break, releasing a collective sigh that no one was injured, and the element of surprise was still on their side.

An hour later, they stumbled into camp, just as the horizon was beginning to blush. It was nearly four. Andy was looking forward to a little sleep before their next round.

Peterson grinned as he collected the two phones. "Great work, gents. I think we made some fans tonight."

Qwanme took possession of the delicate Invisios so he could disinfect, clean, and store them for next use.

"Can't wait to hear what they make of the pictures. Did you see any vehicles up there?" Peterson asked.

"No sir," answered Dallas. "I think they're dropping in supplies. The crater wall going up is so rocky and treacherous, it's a natural barrier. No way could you haul anything heavy in there, so I think it's dropped by chopper."

"Did they all look like kids?"

"Couldn't see," answered Andy. "Might have been a mixed group, but I didn't see any girls, did you guys?"

Kit and Connor shook their heads.

"Saw spent cartridges all over the place," Sven added. "I think it's like a little training camp. Little boys volunteered or abducted to train. They get them old enough to be able to hold and shoot without it sending them back on their butts. An army of children." Sven spat into the night.

"How was *your* day? Train any baboons?" Andy asked Peterson.

"Gunnar had a fit when he discovered his labor crew was gone. You owe the boys who stayed behind some serious bank. And you should have seen Conley.

He was patching up scrapes and bruises and took care of someone's ingrown toenail. Pretty disgusting stuff."

"Yeah, well, when you're trained to operate, you operate," said Andy, laughing to himself. He'd have to give Conley kudos for his good behavior. "And no baboons located or brought into surgery."

"They have to get the pens built first," added Sven. "But you don't want to hear all that screaming all night long. The pack will follow a captured member for miles and make everyone miserable they make such a ruckus."

"I'm gonna take a shower and get this shit off my face. Can I get some shut-eye?" Archie asked.

Peterson nodded and gave the all clear to the group, who scattered. He stepped up to Andy. "You want to go into town today?"

It wasn't the first thing Andy was looking forward to. But the unspoken benefits of that mission was a chance to call Aimee. And he needed to do that.

"Can I get a couple of hours in?"

"Sure. Take three or four. Get some grub and then we'll take off. Today we'll travel by truck.

"I'd like that, sir."

Andy was headed to his cot when Peterson called him out. "Hey, Andy. You did good today. I made sure to tell Kyle you were a very welcome addition here. I think with you on the Team, we're about to change our luck, and I told him so."

"Thank you, sir. But Kyle's not the one I have to

impress. I'd appreciate a good word with the Lt. Commander, sir."

"I'll do that."

As Andy tried to leave, Peterson interrupted him again. He hated like hell when someone didn't know when the conversation was over. He was tired, wet and a little sore. He'd have been happier with a firefight. Sven had been right about that.

"Sir?"

"Do you still think we need Tucker and some of the other guys?"

"Couldn't hurt. I think you're going to have to split the team up into groups to find where they're holding them. It's a huge area we have to search. If it will speed up the mission, I'm all for it. I mean, I think it would be smart to do that."

"I'm glad you said that, because they're on their way. They'll be here in two days."

"Tucker must be a new papa again. That's great." Andy was elated, but knew Tucker was sacrificing much to tag along.

But it was good news. Things were about to get interesting, which either meant they'd pull off a huge rescue mission, or things would go all to hell. But it would be nice to do it with some of his buds.

CHAPTER 13

AIMEE WENT TO the Pinellas County Sheriff's Department and filed an incident report, like Dr. Denby had suggested. One of the deputies knew Andy and several of the other guys on other teams she didn't know. She felt it brought a little extra diligence on their part. They explained that with the report on file, any responding officers hopefully would access it, and thus have better detail on her brother. That meant there was a greater chance less force would be used in any apprehension. She thanked them, got cards and cell phone numbers, and was promised house patrols on a regular basis, particularly at night.

She called Shelley on her way over to the clinic in Largo where she was going to attend a NAMI meeting, which Dr. Denby had also suggested, texting her the location and the fact that there was a day meeting she might be able to make.

"You were right, Shelley. And I just wanted you to

know Dr. Denby was able to put it in terms I could understand. I'm sorry if I was a bit testy with you."

"My bedside manner sucks sometimes. And maybe I just don't have the big heart like you do, but I was worried about it. Still am, Aimee. But you're on the right track."

"Thanks. So, no cop-calling, okay? I'm going to be in that meeting, so don't panic."

Shelley laughed. "I'm going over to the school to start getting the classroom set up for after break. You want to catch dinner somewhere, or do you need some space?"

"No, actually I was thinking the same thing. I'll text you when I'm done. Let's make it an early dinner, okay?"

"You got it. Can I ask you if Andy has called?"

Aimee sighed into the phone, feeling that tiny stab of pain and worry again. "Not yet. It's still early. I'm not worried," she lied.

"Okay, I promise not to ask again. See you later."

She had an hour before the meeting began, so she visited the Rose Hill Shelter. It was a training school for vet techs, and she'd driven by it hundreds of times, and never thought about adoption before.

The reception area was sterile, and of course there was the unmistakable smell of animals, even though it was clean, and the floor buffed to a shiny patina. The walls were papered with posters of missing pets or stories of how abandoned dogs and cats had been adopted, some of them with major injuries, and went on to have a happy, normal life afterwards. Aimee drew strength and hope from the many stories advertised there.

A young, uniformed technician asked her to come forward when her name was called.

"I'd like to inquire about seeing some of your dogs who need good homes. I've never done this before. What's the process?"

"Do you have a preference for size of dog?"

"I would think a larger one. I don't want a puppy. They're cute, but I think too much work for me."

"Have you had a dog before?"

"When I was growing up. Our family had a lab mix of some kind. Her name was Cookie. My parents had her for about ten years."

The tech went on to explain the process and told her that many of the dogs who were deemed receptive had gone through simple obedience training and were house broken. Many of the dogs had been left behind by elderly people undergoing life changes, so it wasn't uncommon to find a dog already very well behaved and desiring human companionship.

The hardest part of the meeting was seeing the variety of dog population in cages. Aimee wanted to take them all. One by one, she put her fingers up to the cage and spoke with several. The technician let her interact with three who she felt a connection with, so she had a short playtime in one of the rooms.

There was a beautiful golden retriever mix named Sandy who looked like she had the youth and energy to be able to take on runs. Her bark was loud, but she was also very playful. The dog had been spayed already and hadn't been in the shelter long. She went over the dog's records with the tech, and Aimee was hopeful Andy would be okay with her decision.

Sandy sat in front of her as she explained her situation to the young girl. "I need to check with my husband first, and I should get a call in the next few days. I want to be sure he's okay with having a dog, since this isn't anything we've talked about. Can I reserve her for a few days? Get back to you?"

Sandy put a paw on her lap as if she understood. She was begging to be taken home.

"I can call you if someone else comes in and wants to adopt her. We do charge a fee, so if you pay the deposit, I can give you first right. But if we don't hear back from you within a few hours, then we'll release the dog to someone else. I think she's very adoptable and won't be here long, so don't take too much time."

As Aimee said good-bye, Sandy's mournful expression broke her heart. She knew the look the dog gave her as she was being led back to her cage was something she'd never forget. She was already connected and ready to take the plunge.

The clinic in Largo was an outpatient drop in space servicing runaways and teens. She smelled fresh coffee brewing and knew that usually meant a meeting was about to begin, so followed her nose to a large class-room with chairs around several long tables. About a dozen people had already arrived, some in pairs and some singles.

Aimee was greeted and given a name badge, after being introduced to several of the regular attendees. By the time the meeting coordinator arrived, nearly all the seats had been filled.

She was introduced again as a newcomer, on behalf of her brother. Aimee was grateful she didn't have to go into details of her relationship with Logan with a room full of strangers. She listened to stories from parents, siblings and even spouses of people affected by various forms of mental illness. Some were kids living on the street that parents hadn't seen for many years. Others were trying to cope with a family member living in their house, disrupting other family or worse, stealing and abusing others. One couple had a daughter diagnosed with a severe mental illness they had dealt with for several years, only to find out that their other child, a son, also had the same disease diagnosed recently.

Aimee heard the stories of mothers who loved their

sons and daughters, but who were afraid of their own children. They had stories of sending them to expensive rehab clinics. People had lost homes trying to pay for their kids' addiction issues over and over again until the family was near homeless themselves.

She heard one tale of a mother who hadn't seen her son for ten years but looked for him everywhere. She'd volunteered at homeless shelters, just to be able to have some sight of him, but never had and was still waiting.

It was an eye-opening experience for her. The room was filled with hope, with realism, but she found a family of people there who were going through exactly what she was with Logan.

The coordinator asked her, finally, if she wanted to share about her experiences.

"My brother, Logan, has been homeless for over twelve years now, maybe longer, I don't know. We grew up in California, so when I moved here, I was surprised to see him working in a restaurant one night. But I could never get in touch with him. He was fired the night I saw him, and when I looked into where he was staying, he'd left his program and was back out on the street."

She showed them the gift he had left her. A couple of ladies were crying as she told her story. Then she talked about how conflicted she was about what to do with his reaching out and got more personal stories, all mixed, of how that had worked out for others in the room.

"Main thing is to make sure you don't put yourself in harm's way, Aimee," the coordinator said. "I think from what you've heard today, you can expect that it will be a long bumpy road. Even when they clean up, they are still very flawed. You have to understand it's a long process and sometimes without a perfect ending."

Aimee was grateful for the honesty. She walked away knowing that there wasn't one size fits all solutions to these problems and that if she was going to bring Logan into their lives together, it was a long row to hoe. It was important to her that she let Andy know what she'd discovered so it could be a joint description.

But the funny thing was that, of all the stories that were told, all the questions anyone had in the group, everyone was completely aligned that Aimee should adopt Sandy and not wait for Andy's permission.

She took a class schedule and learned about a series of lectures given by various health professionals, helping to bring mental illness the attention it deserved, and vowed she'd attend as many of them as she could.

On the way home, she nearly went by the shelter and picked Sandy up, but held to her conviction that she ask Andy first.

All during dinner she thought about the golden

dog who had so stolen her heart. The more she thought about it, the more convinced she became that adopting Sandy was the right thing to do. Shelley was happy to hear about the group and the classes.

"But I'm going to insist that you not stay home alone until you get that dog, Aimee. You're welcome to stay with me."

"I'm fine, Shelley, really."

"There you go again. Then invite me over. Honestly, Aimee, I won't sleep a wink if you don't."

"Okay. I'm in the mood for some romantic movies anyway. We'll get out the Kleenex and have a good cry tonight."

"Oh dear. That bad?"

"Well, you're inviting yourself. Are you sure you want to come?"

"Maybe we should work on a puzzle."

"Nope, it's going to be the Romance Channel. I want to learn about broken hearts that are mended, things that turn out in the end just the way we want them to. I've had enough reality for one day. And then I'm going to cry myself to sleep and dream of my husband."

Shelley shook her head in mock disgust. Finally, she added, with a wry smile, "Okay, but if you touch me, I'll slap you so hard, you'll see stars."

CHAPTER 14

T HE ROAD TO Benot twisted through some beautiful scenery, showing sparkling lakes and little villages tucked into the foliage along the edges. Life was simple there. The colorful patterns of dresses and headdress the ladies wore were fascinating to Andy. They passed by women working in the fields, or drying animal skins and boiling fabric in huge oil drum kettles. Everywhere there was a healthy population of chickens and toddlers.

Peterson had told them their cover was that they were helping to set up a clinic in the town, given a charter through a church charity in the states. Sven thought that approach was a sound one. They were out scouting for locations to set up shop.

"Everything in the big city needs permission. That way we find out who is running it. Who is afraid of whom, who the good guys are and who are not so good."

Sven had taken the seat next to Andy.

"So you heard Tucker's coming."

"Yup, so is Armando, Fredo, and Kelly is on her way too, plus a couple others. I'm hoping there will be some guys from Colin Riley's new concern. I'm anxious to talk to them, see how they're doing."

"So you and Kelly might patch things up?" Andy asked.

"We'll see. I haven't spoken to her. I'm keeping a low profile. But I'm glad she's coming. She has the best kind of connections."

"So, is she still independent."

"She got her credentials back. Can't explain how she got them in such quick order because normally they take weeks. Somebody high up must have pulled some strings."

"Maybe Riley had something to do with it."

Sven wrinkled his nose. "State is sometimes difficult. They aren't elected officials who could use a campaign donation. So I don't think Riley has the pull there. But this mission got on someone's radar, so I'm grateful."

"Those diplomatic connections might come in handy."

"I hope we don't need them, but yes." Sven watched a group of young girls walking home from school, all in a dark blue and white uniform. Two nuns sat nearby drinking a can of soda nearby, under the shade of an umbrella.

"You don't see many of those here, do you?" Andy asked Sven.

"Not hardly. Used to be heavily catholic, but not so much. Everything takes a back seat to politics these days. They've lost so many clergy in the past few years. And the UN cannot make up the shortfall, but they're trying."

"So, will we be welcomed here?"

"Hard to say. First, we'll try it without Kelly. If we strike out, we'll come back with her and let her work her magic." Sven winked, and gave a belly laugh. Andy knew he was looking forward to the reunion and the magic she might bring to his life too.

Peterson turned in the front seat, addressing them. "Andy, I promised you a call home. What about you, Sven?"

"Thanks, sir. I'm good."

His LPO handed Andy the phone. "Wait until we come to a stop. I'll give you about five minutes privacy, and then you join us, got it?"

"Thanks, man."

The quaintness of the countryside was soon diluted with evidence of a city coming up. The road widened, and was also littered with abandoned cars, a dead chicken that had been run over, and scooters buzzing in and around traffic everywhere, making the driving especially challenging. Andy's neck was beginning to hurt from the jerking movements of their truck. He'd gotten some bites on his legs that itched badly and were swollen. He was going to look for some Benadryl as soon as he could safely get his kit out.

Several taller buildings clustered around a central location of the town, with a fountain at the intersection of two main roads. Children played in the pool, splashing cars and tossing water through opened truck windows and pedestrian traffic passing by. The red clay from the dusty non-paved thoroughfare had scattered silt everywhere. Andy was beginning to taste it.

The driver pulled into a parking lot outside a commercial bank building several stories tall. Peterson directed the other two trucks to pull up alongside them while everyone got out, adjusted their packs and stretched their legs. The driver had promised to watch their stuff, but no one was buying it.

Andy dialed Aimee's number. If it was Noon in Africa, it would be around five in the morning Florida time. But she picked her phone up after two rings.

"God it's good to hear your voice, sweetheart," Andy started.

"Me too, Andy. I kept telling myself to be patient. It wasn't working. So glad you called."

"Listen, I've only been given five minutes so let's

make it count. I'm good, it's hot, the food is passable, mostly what we pack in here, so far there is no end in sight, but I'm safe. Settling in. Anything eventful going on there?"

"Oh, God, where do I start?"

"Uh Oh. Hope that doesn't mean Cory's making a nuisance of himself."

"No. Haven't seen him, but I think Logan has been reaching out to me. Made me a bracelet and left it on the doorstep. I gave him some of your old clothes."

"Is that necessary? I mean, not that I'm in love with the clothes, but do you think that's wise?"

"I've been told that. And you'll be happy to know Shelley and Dr. Denby got me to file a police report."

"You're welcome, Andy," Shelley's voice shouted from the other side of the room.

"Shelley's staying over? That's smart. Tell her thanks."

"I'm learning about mental illness. Dr. Denby suggested a group, and I attended the first meeting today."

"This isn't one of those twelve step programs now, is it?"

"No, it's a support group."

"Okay. So you filed a police report. And, what else? How does Logan look?"

"I haven't seen him, Andy. I just know it's him."

"Okay, that explains why Shelley's there."

"I want to ask you something. I want to adopt a dog. It was suggested since I'm alone so much. But I wanted to get your approval first."

"He better be potty trained."

"I found a really nice golden Lab mix. I think she'd be a good running companion too. But mainly it's for my safety. I don't know how he found out where we live, but with a loyal dog, I'd feel safer."

"I'm cool with it." Andy saw Peterson give him the wrap up signal. "Hey, I gotta go. I'll try to call back in a couple of days. But promise me you'll not encourage him to hang around the house Aimee, okay? Not without me there."

"Do you know how long?"

"No clue."

"One more quick question. If I need to talk to someone, do I call your LPO's wife on Team 4, or—"

"Call Christy. What do you need to talk about?"

"I don't know. There's a lot more going on. Met with Carmen Hernandez and her attorney—"

"Problems? Okay, look, I'm really getting pressured. But call Christy. Use her. They aren't on deployment yet, so you can even talk to Kyle if you want."

"Thanks. Go save the day."

"Working on it."

Peterson banged on the window and yelled from

behind the glass, "Carr! I need your butt out here, now."

Andy was embarrassed Aimee had to hear that. He also didn't think it was very smart for him to make such a spectacle or draw attention to them.

"Sorry, Andy. Love you. Be safe."

"Love you, sweetheart. Sleep naked, but not when Shelley's over there."

She was still laughing when Andy hung up.

Peterson grabbed the phone back. "Next time, three minutes, then maybe you'll be done in five."

"Sorry. You know how it is with that first phone call home."

They divided into two groups of six. Andy stayed with Sven and Dallas went with Peterson. They were to work the perimeter of the town center, looking for a space large enough for a three-office clinic, or that was the ruse. But while they were checking out vacant buildings for lease, they were observing the population, other shops and who ran them.

"Everything okay at home?" Sven asked.

"More or less. Being married is complicated. It's good, don't get me wrong, but Aimee gets into things and I'd just feel better being there."

"That's always the way it happens. Shit explodes sometimes at home."

"This wasn't that bad, but—well that's a talk for

another time when I don't have to concentrate."

They took pictures of storefronts but also got shots of the local Guarda police, and license plates of some expensive cars slowly traveling through the downtown area. Even the shops on the ground floor level were of interest. Several times they found a group of military-aged males gathering in the back of some of these shops or walking together on the opposite street. The team observed what kind of vehicles they drove, and who they talked to.

The two groups met back near their parked trucks. Sven had a plan to talk to the local Commissioner of Health, so while the rest of the team waited, he and Andy and Peterson walked up the steps to a three-story government office. At the side in a taller wing, was the local jail, evident by the bars on the windows. Faces appeared between the bars along with hands, and forearms as the prisoners watched the streets below.

Inside, the building was air conditioned, which was such a welcome that Andy closed his eyes and took in a deep breath of cool, clean air free of red clay dust. Sven had already opened the frosted glass door to Amadi Sabi's office, the Commissioner of Health.

They were lucky to find Mr. Sabi sitting behind his desk, the reception area of his office vacant. He motioned for them to enter his office, saying something in his local Benin tongue. As they entered through the doorway, he switched to French, having sized them up to be Europeans.

Sven spoke up, responding in French, and asked if he spoke English.

"Yes, yes I do. You are English then?"

"I'm Norwegian, but these two are from the States, yes. Allow me to introduce you. This is Dr. Carr, and Dr. Peterson. We are here from the Southern Baptist Africa Project. We've been given a mandate to find a suitable location to set up a mobile clinic. We'll need a base office, and Benot is centrally located."

"Please, sit down," he said graciously. There was only one chair across from his desk, so Peterson took it. Andy hoped they didn't look too rough around the edges, since they had been literally camping in the bush for four days. Sven continued the discussion.

"We understand this is a safe area?" he floated to Mr. Sabi, trying to calculate the rise he'd get out of the gentleman.

Sabi laughed deep and long—almost a guttural growl—shaking his head. "If you wanted safe, well then you'd have to go back to the States. But even there it isn't safe. But here, in Africa, we are very grateful for what the rest of the world can do to help us. We welcome you with open arms. I can probably find some surplus properties you can rent direct from this office, saving you from having to deal with crooked leasing agents in town. How does that sound?"

"Well, what I meant was, we'd like to make a presence here, expand if we could. Perhaps build a hospital," Sven proposed.

"You have such strength?"

"We do a lot of fundraising. For the right cause, yes."

"I cannot promise you a site for a hospital, but if you want to operate a clinic, you would have to do so under my office auspices. And we wouldn't want to interfere with the World Health projects in the area, either. For instance, we wouldn't want to build a clinic right next to another one, would we? We'd like to serve the entire country."

"That makes sense, Mr. Sabi. Where would be the greatest need in the safest area?"

"Look, doctor—what did you say your name was?"

"I am not a doctor. Sven Tolar."

"Mr. Tolar from Norway, the safest place is one that is well guarded. You see, the way we work here is that we provide you with a good location at a relatively cheap price, but you will have to hire security to ensure the integrity of the project and keep the doors open. Many of our police and fire departments work extra duty as guards in banks, hospitals, clinics and sometimes schools, or traveling with businessmen and officials from all around the world."

"So what you're telling me is that the location isn't as important, as long as we have the budget for the security, right?"

"Exactly."

"And what if we were to bring our own security?" Peterson injected.

"Of course, but they would work under our people, who are highly trained and specialize in knowing everything there is to know about security here. You wouldn't want to do it on your own. It's not recommended, and I don't think I could get the permits for it, either."

Andy felt Sven had come to the end of his useful conversation. In one hand, Sabi had a sheaf of papers at least a quarter inch thick.

"So you wish we should fill out the paperwork?" Andy asked, leaning forward to accept the stack of forms.

"Please, doctor," he said, handing them to Andy.

When Peterson stood, Mr. Sabi did as well, shaking their hands one by one. "Gentlemen, I look forward to our partnership going forward. Please, use me as your resource. I will help you get whatever you need. I will be your partner, standing in the shadows, making things happen for you. All worries about security and safety should by now be put to rest. N'est pas?"

CHAPTER 15

S HELLEY WAS OFF to her classroom prep so the two parted company and went their separate ways. Aimee couldn't wait to go get Sandy. On the way, she stopped for a set of stainless steel dog bowls in their own stand, bought dog treats and some expensive gourmet frozen raw dog food with venison and salmon, along with some kibbles. She also bought a yellow jeweled collar and hoped it would fit, with a yellow leash to match. The pet store owner recommended a good shampoo for a longer-haired dog, and she passed on the conditioner.

The whole bill was just under two hundred dollars. She swallowed hard and gave her credit card.

With the new leash and collar clutched in her hand, she ran up the steps and into the reception area. A new clerk was at the front desk.

"I'm here to pick up Sandy."

"Sandy? Let me check to see if she's still here. We

had a couple in here yesterday afternoon, and I thought they adopted her."

Aimee was crestfallen.

"But I paid the deposit. She said they would hold her for me for a few days, and call me first if—"

"I see that she's been adopted. I'm so sorry."

"But—" Aimee's eyes began to overflow. She looked down at the leash and the collar and felt the pangs deep in her heart. "I *paid* for her."

"No one pays, Miss."

It was a snooty answer, but Aimee knew she had it coming. Suddenly, the helpful tech was looking ugly and cruel. Aimee wanted to climb over the counter and go check for herself to make sure the dog was really gone. But then she'd have to see all those other lonesome faces behind bars—sweet animals she couldn't afford to take home.

The tech was waiting for Aimee to say something further.

"Can't you double check with your colleague who was here yesterday? Do you actually have adoption paperwork processed?"

The girl's eyes narrowed. "I don't have access to the Director's office and he keeps all the adoption files there. But yes, I see that her fee was paid and—"

"But *I* paid the fee. *I* did it," Aimee insisted.

"It happens all the time. Some people come in and

pay for an animal and then just never come pick it up." Her eyebrows, that tiny strip of over-plucked hair above her eyes rose into her bangs.

Aimee was horrified. "Can you check to see if she's still here?"

Just then, the girl from yesterday entered the reception area, wearing a rubber apron and gloves. She pushed the hair from her forehead and greeted Aimee.

"I'd shake your hand, but—"

"She's come for Sandy," the other tech whispered.

"Yes, and I got her all bathed for you. I had a feeling you'd be by. And since we've had so much interest in her, I knew someone would be taking her soon if you didn't. So I pulled her paperwork."

Aimee nearly fainted with relief.

"That's why she doesn't show up on the list," she said to the other girl.

"Okay, well then I'm going to go get the exercise group going. Can you finish with her?"

"Of course." The tech smiled at Aimee. "I'm so sorry about that. I can see you were close to a meltdown. That bodes well for Sandy."

"I couldn't stop thinking about her. I talked to my husband early this morning, and he was fine with it. I knew she'd be popular."

"You made a wise choice, although we try to get the right homes for all our animals here. Some of our most injured ones, the ones who need the most care and love, seem to find the most loving homes. It's really a labor of love working here. There are special people all over the Largo area—they even come from out of state to check out our dogs. Sandy's profile just went up on our website yesterday and we've had lots of calls. But that just means another nice dog will be adopted, so it's all good."

"Thank you, for what you do. When I have an opportunity, and I can't do it now, I'd love to make a donation to your shelter. You're a non-profit?

"Yes, and since we're aligned with the school, we keep our fees low since it is offset a bit from part of their tuition, so it helps." She removed her rubber gloves and apron, tossing them in a towel bin in the corner. "Now, let's get the paperwork done and then we'll see if the pretty girl is all ready for you. I don't want to put her in your car if she's still wet."

"I don't care. I honestly don't." Aimee knew Andy would have something to say about the condition of the car afterwards, but that was a hurdle she'd have to mount later. Right now, all she wanted to do was get Sandy to her home and get her adjusted seamlessly.

The tech helped Aimee fill out the adoption paperwork. She was given a form she'd have to fill out to get her dog license, but the fee was included in her payment. In her paperwork was a list of vets in the area, and a copy of what shots she'd had, and she was up to date. There was an extra copy so Aimee could send it in with the license form.

"Can I ask you a favor? If I fill this out, can you send it in for me? That way I know it will be done correctly. Add the shot records too?"

"Absolutely." She began filling in several boxes and then turned it over to Aimee to put her address and signature at the bottom. "I'll include a copy of the license charge, and you might want to put in your cell number."

"Oh, good idea." Aimee added that.

"One more thing? Go to one of those pet stores that has the address tags, and fill in your address and your phone number, in case she gets lost. It helps. She's going to be a little skittish at first, since everything's new, so you should get this done on your way home. Your license should be mailed to you within a week or so."

"Thank you so much!"

"Okay, well, I'm going to get your girl, see if she's ready."

Aimee handed her the leash and the collar.

"Oh this is cute. A jeweled collar. I can tell she's going to be spoiled."

"No doubt about it."

The tech disappeared behind a swinging door while

Aimee tapped her foot. She heard her stomach growl and realized she hadn't eaten anything for breakfast. Someone else came into the room behind her, which set off a little bell summoning an attendant, but Aimee could take her eyes off that little crack in the door, waiting.

At last, she heard the tech's voice behind the door, "That's a good girl. Now, let's go outside and meet your new mommy, shall we?"

Right on que, Sandy barked. Aimee was so thrilled she nearly wet her pants. Sandy burst through the door, and ran right for her, yanking the leash from the tech's hand. She put her paws on the counter and barked again.

Aimee leaned forward. "We're going to have to teach you about that, but are you ready to go home?"

The dog fed on the excitement of the moment. Aimee figured she was conditioned by the sight of the leash, and not necessarily going home with her. But she'd take whatever she could get. She reached over the countertop, grabbed the leash as the tech popped up the countertop to allow Sandy to enter the reception area. But Sandy was headed straight for the door, no doubt excited to be taken for a walk.

The tech followed behind, all the paperwork stuck in a plastic bag, along with some instructions and a couple dog treats. Aimee opened the second door, and

Sandy jumped in on the seat without being coaxed.

"You're going to need to get a seat cover. This dog is going to shed," said the young girl.

"I know it. And I'm going to need a dog bed too. I tried to think of everything. I'll get it on the way home."

The tech gave a loving rub to Sandy's jowl, patted her head, and accepted the paw she was presented, shaking it. "Good-bye, Sandy. Have fun in your new home."

Aimee closed the door, and by the time she went around to the driver's seat, Sandy had already occupied it. She slid herself in and ordered the dog to go to the back seat, which she did. With a thumbs up, Aimee drove out of the parking lot and headed for the pet store on the way home.

AFTER ANOTHER TWO-HUNDRED-DOLLAR shopping spree, even with the pet store owner giving her a ten percent discount on her new purchases, Aimee and Sandy were finally home. She attached her leash and tried not to let her pull too hard, yanking it back sharply to get the dog to heal. She figured it wasn't too soon to begin training. Once inside the door, she unclipped the leash and let the dog roam the house, while she brought in the food, the dog bed and the treats.

When Aimee entered the living room, she didn't see Sandy anywhere.

"Sandy? Where are you?"

Did I leave the door open?

Dropping her items, she ran up the stairs to the master bedroom. Sandy had ensconced herself, nestled in the pillows of her bed. That's when Aimee knew she could take the dog bed back. That's where the dog was used to sleeping when she had an owner who loved her.

"Well, if that's the way it's going to be, Sandy, I'll be fine with it. But you're going to have to sell Andy on the idea. He's going to be your biggest problem."

Sandy angled her head, listening, as if she understood fully.

CHAPTER 16

ANDY HELPED THE cranky UN project manager to build sheds and enclosures for his new project. He put up with the eccentric former zookeeper, but it wasn't long before he realized the man really did know quite a bit about primates. The long term mission wasn't as important as helping to gain his trust and support today. They were using the jungle outpost as their new base, even though they had a perfectly good one closer to the Northern border. They owed him something.

The photographs that had been taken proved that indeed there was a training camp for young boys at the top of Mont Sokbaro. What wasn't clear was who was paying for this, and without complaints of kidnappings or the abuse of the children, the folks in Norfolk decided it was something they should not insert themselves in. At least for now.

That suited Andy fine.

So, the search remained for the hostages, and every day now that it wasn't resolved was creating a lot of tension. The upper brass decided the Team should remain at Gunnar's encampment, but continue to work their way outward in all directions, like the spokes of a wheel, sweeping through the grassy savannah lands, trying to get information from some of the smaller villages since the larger towns were proving to be dry holes. These were mostly farmers, who tended small plots and sold their goods locally at the markets. Life was simple, and it was also very tough. They had a natural distrust of newcomers and strangers which often brought so much violence with them.

It was a good decision, based on good intel and Andy agreed it could yield fruit, given enough time.

They had a two-day window until Tucker and Kelly arrived, along with several others from Kyle's SEAL Team 3, and that reunion was to be back at the stone-walled villa near Kandi and the Niger border they'd been taken to their first day here.

Sometimes drone footage would highlight something interesting they'd send a party to the next day, but no one was coming up with any actionable result, until the day they were supposed to leave for the rendezvous up North. A girl's school in Benot had been attacked and two teachers and a half dozen girls were taken. From the way the attack occurred, Peterson, Sven and Dallas were convinced it was the same group.

"They came in with guns blazing, killing the local police who were moonlighting as guards at the school. Once the protectors were gone, they were able to grab at random," said Peterson. "We're to go looking for them."

"What about Tucker and the others we're supposed to meet?" asked Andy.

"I guess we'll be late, then," said Peterson. "This takes priority now. We'll get up there as soon as we can."

"Or, maybe a few of us could go up and bring them down to meet us here," Sven added.

"Yeah, it doesn't make much sense to have people who can help sitting on their hands," said Dallas.

"Problem as I see it is, we can't spare anybody." Peterson's jaw was set. He was about to make a big mistake and all three of the others knew it.

This was one of those times where an LPO earned his creds or lost the confidence of the team. Andy knew there were always dangers to every decision. Picking the right choice to navigate the best one was hard, but what a good leader had to learn to do.

"Look, why don't Sven and I go up there and get them. We take one truck. Sven knows the road. We can get back down here quickly if we don't hike like we did coming in." Andy was hoping Peterson would buy it but could already see he was set against splitting the Team up any further.

"Not what I'd do. You're gonna have to stick with me for a bit. We'll get up there, and just a couple of days won't make that much difference."

Dallas spat on the ground but held his tongue.

Andy thought about the choice again, and what was about to be done, and decided to lay it on the line. He didn't want to give Peterson a challenge to his authority, but he knew it was a mistake. Convinced Tucker and Kelly, as well as the others they brought would double their chances of a successful mission, he had to speak out.

"I'm going to ask you to consider something, sir." Andy saw Peterson's eyes go red with anger, and then settle down, as the fear factor started percolating.

"All right. Let's hear it. But then I decide and that's the end of it, agreed?"

Everyone nodded their heads.

"Sven and I are part of the Team, but newbies. We add an extra element to the mix. The guys haven't worked with us much yet. You've already got a full squad. You've got Conley, several others speak French. You met with Mr. Sabi—it would be easy to add someone to that conversation. But, if we stay, and just say it doesn't work out how we think it should, say we engage and it gets heavy, you think any of us would be able to send two out to get the rest of the team that, at that point, we'd sorely need? But, if we delay and you guys do general information gathering and not execute the spear until we have a full force, we'll have better intel, and a whole lot more firepower. It's just nuts to have them waiting up there."

Silence took over the group. Dallas jumped in.

"Two more won't be as effective as the seven we have on the way. Weakest link in that plan is, what happens if you or Sven get into trouble? Then we're totally cut off, and the groups stay separated or go in blind."

Andy nodded at the obvious flaw in his plan and got Sven's attention. "What do you think?" he asked the Norwegian.

"I like it. Can we take one of the Gunnar's guys? Part of his corps? Might give us legitimacy."

"You're gonna get that bastard to give up one of his men? What planet are you on, Sven?" Peterson was livid with that suggestion.

Sven coolly tilted his head and smiled. Andy knew he'd already thought about the solution.

"Well, we tell him that we're going up to get Uncle Sam's money, and his State Department liaison, who will be very grateful for his assistance and might make a serious donation to his cause. It could lighten his heavy financial burden, a bit."

Dallas began to chuckle. Andy had a hard time keeping a straight face, so he looked at his boots.

"You son of a bitch. How do you know they're bringing in cash?" Peterson demanded.

"Because that's part of what Kelly does. And she's got the backing of a billionaire, too. And I was in on the rescue of his daughter last year. He'd do just about anything to find these guys. If she doesn't bring some in, she can get it quickly."

It was a beautiful plan. Andy could see that Peterson was hesitant to make a decision.

"You know in your gut it's the only way, sir. It risks only two of us, but damn if it doesn't increase the odds by double. I'm willing to put my life on the line for it. Sven here is dumb enough to do anything."

Dallas started to laugh.

Andy continued, "Besides, you can always say Sven talked you into it later, if you have to."

"But I don't want to have that conversation with the Headshed."

"With all due respect, sir, I don't know a good LPO who hasn't," grumbled Dallas.

Andy had been told stories about Kyle. "As legendary as Lansdowne is, there was a time in his career he thought he was going to be written up and stuck on a desk, or worse. It was a real rough patch, and it lasted months."

"I heard about that," whispered Dallas. "I think my brother was on the team when that went down."

Sven put his arm on Peterson's shoulder. "There are no safe choices, only good ones. You're about to make a really good one, Peterson. And us three are going to help you carry it out. Put your trust in us."

It started as a gentle nod of his head, but within seconds, Peterson was completely focused on saying yes. "Hell, let's go for it."

It wouldn't have been appropriate to cheer, but Andy thought he heard one echoing out over the lush savannah grasslands of Benin, something he might have heard in any football stadium back home.

One of the things he'd been taught by SEALs who had gone before him was that it was a very good idea to make your LPO look damn smart, and that kudos and promotions always ran downward to the benefit of the men underneath. Not to mention, this was the Brotherhood. A team was supposed to cover all the aspects of a mission, making up for little weaknesses that would inevitably pop up. They were prepared to do the impossible. It was what their training was all about. It was what the Trident meant, after all. If the roles were reversed, and Andy was the LPO, they'd all do the same for him.

CHAPTER 17

AIMEE TOOK SANDY out for a run on Gulf Boulevard, eventually winding up at the nearby dog park. There, she was able to let her off the leash and let her run freely, playing with several others.

She checked her cell and returned a call to Mr. Kornblum.

"I'm afraid I have some bad news. Carmen passed away last night. It was very peaceful I'm told."

Aimee's nerve endings were stunted as this new bombshell scattered at her feet. She sat forward, clutching the phone to her ear so she could hear better.

"But she looked so—" It was hard to accept after only knowing her for such a short time. Her passing brought on a wave of regret. Although she'd been told this might happen, it wasn't something she expected so soon.

"I know. I was a little surprised myself. But the doctors had been warning me all along this could happen.

But, like you, I was not expecting it for perhaps weeks. So, now I have the task of administering her trust, filing notices and distributing her assets according to her will. And that involves you, Aimee, as the sole beneficiary. Is it possible you could meet me in the office tomorrow, or sometime this week?"

"Gosh, everything is so rushed these days for me—changing so fast I can hardly keep track. I just met her, and now she's gone. I'm being selfish, I know."

"Not at all, Aimee. Perfectly normal. But I'm glad you acted when you did. Take your time, if you like. There isn't any time requirement, but it's always more prudent to do it sooner than later. Sometimes, in these cases, people start coming out of the woodwork, claiming they're entitled to a piece of the estate. I have no such knowledge of anyone like that, but I never say never. However, the will is pretty bullet-proof, if I do say so myself."

"Oh gosh. I didn't think of that. Really?"

"Happens all the time. But that's not your worry. It's mine to protect. Just remember, this is what she wanted, Aimee."

She gulped in air. "Okay, I could be there tomorrow if—" she looked at Sandy playing. She didn't dare leave her in the house alone. It was too soon.

"If what?"

"I adopted a dog, and I've just picked her up today.

Would it be possible for me to bring her with me? I don't trust that she can be left in my house alone."

"What kind of dog?"

"She's big. Retriever mix. But well behaved. I don't think she'd cause a problem."

"I don't see why not. I have clients with service dogs all the time. So, tomorrow, shall we say ten o'clock?"

Aimee knew she didn't have to check her calendar. Several of her workmen were just coming back from visiting their families out of state, and no one had called her about coming back just yet. "I'll be there."

She ran with Sandy further down the boulevard, then reversed course and came back to her house. The dog was mildly distracted with the traffic, but overall, she did very well on her first day out. She nearly drained her water dish, so Aimee knew to be on the lookout for her first accident.

The mail came, and books she'd ordered arrived in their brown packaging. Two were Hank Borges books, dog-eared with covers curling up. She sat down bringing her coffee into the living room as Sandy jumped up on the leather couch, nestling beside her as if she'd grown up there.

"Do you like science fiction, Sandy? This man," she held up the book, "used to write books in this very house. He probably wrote this one here. Should we look?"

Sandy's ears were alert, waiting to listen to more of the story.

Opening the cover page, Aimee read the dedication.

This book is dedicated to C, who knows the outer space of my interior better than anyone else in this galaxy. There are epic travels we will take one day, and they will be glorious journeys of the heart. Just think what we can discover when we leave our temporal bodies and free ourselves into the Heavens."

H—

Inside the back cover flap was the familiar black and white picture of Borges standing barefoot on the beach just like the one outside her living room window. She flipped back to the dedication page, and then turned through the list of his books and testimonials, looking for something about or for Carmen, but at last came to the title page, and then the start of the book.

The Prince of Scion.

'It was the summer that would change his life forever. Just one trip to the green waters and yellow beaches of Scion, the mythical healing beach on the fourth planet of the Recovery Galaxy. He

knew that all the energy he received from the ocean would help restore his wounds and make the upcoming battle his to own. He was conqueror of the worlds of Scion. But he'd been ousted.

Now was his chance to come back, with revenge, and this time, he'd win the war.'

Aimee continued reading the story until past the brightest part of the day, and then until the sun began to set. She patted Sandy on the head, and walked out on the beach, clutching Hank Borges' book in her left hand. Checking back at her house, she saw Sandy sitting there just inside the window, watching like a sentry.

The crowds were smaller today, with the air crisp and colder than usual. The waves barely made a noise as they lapped upon the smooth wet sand surface. She waved to the fisherman who was out there every day sitting in his lawn chair, often drinking beers in the morning. She watched as a pod of dolphin swam by, heading south, taking turns breaching the waterline and then diving back in. There was hardly an audience to revel in their beauty.

She'd not been spending much time outside the last few days. The wedding and then Andy's sudden departure made the past week feel like a marathon. They'd spent so much time planning everything, and then in a whoosh it was all over, and she was alone, like the first time she came to Sunset Beach. Then there was poor Carmen, and the bracelet that Logan had left for her. So much had happened there was not enough time to tell Andy about it all.

And now things were about to change again. She thought about Logan and what he was doing, even regretting that she'd filed the police report.

It seemed the whole world was pulling her in a direction not of her choosing. She started the walk, of course, faced the path, but forces unseen were guiding her deeper into the forest, away from former routines, the world she thought she knew so well.

Is this how a new bride feels?

Aimee knew that most brides didn't have to say good-bye to their new husbands not even a week after the marriage. Maybe that's what was causing all her confusion. Everything in her world had begun to shift. It almost felt like she didn't have any control in the matter.

As the sun melted into the horizon, she said her little prayer for Andy, wishing he could feel the pull of the magic of this place, that golden tether bringing him back home safe to her. It would all be over soon, and then they'd be together once again, to jumpstart their future—until the next mission, of course.

Maybe in time this would begin to feel routine.

Aimee fed Sandy again, prepared herself some soup and then made sure everything downstairs was locked. Sandy followed her up the stairs where she jumped back up on the king-sized mattress and waited for her to shower and dress for bed.

She took the book with her, adjusted the pillows and with Sandy by her side, tried to finish the story. She fell away into a green oceans of Scion dream, wondering what was to become of the prince's blue vampire second in command. Would he find a happily ever after, or was this not going to be a romance?

SANDY'S BARK AWAKENED Aimee around one o'clock AM. She clamored to her feet, grabbing her robe. Sandy was at the open doorway to the master, clearly barking at something downstairs. She stepped next to the dog, then came out onto the balcony overlooking the living room area and checking for movement and didn't find anything of interest.

"What did you hear, girl?" she asked as she pet the top of her head. Sandy stood on all fours, wagging her tail, but didn't appear to want to go downstairs.

"Should we try it?" Aimee called out, "Is there anyone there?" Her voice echoed throughout the great room. They both listened carefully. There was no answer.

Andy kept a baseball bat in the guest bedroom,

which she passed on her way to the landing. She grabbed it, and with Sandy by her side, made her way silently down the stairs, barefoot and vigilant, her arm raised high, just in case.

As she approached the front entryway, Sandy whined, which made Aimee stop.

"Who's there? Is there someone out there?"

Again, there was no answer. She pointed to the door and asked Sandy to go check it out. The dog ran right up to it, barked several times and sat looking at it, perfectly still, listening.

The hair on the back of her neck began to spike. She felt sweat running down her armpits and her mouth was chalky and parched.

"Who's there?" she shouted and waited, hearing nothing. Aimee approached the door and put her ear to it. She heard nothing but the sounds of an occasional car on Gulf Boulevard. A bundle of leaves blew around outside in a sudden gust. The door was still locked. She glanced around the room, and after determining she was alone, reached for the door and turned the handle, unlocking it.

Sandy came to standing position, wagging her tail.

"Who is it, girl? Do you know who it is?"

She continued wagging her tail, anxious for her to open the door. And so she did.

The dog burst out into the carport several feet,

stopped and sniffed the air. Aimee had followed her onto the stoop, but again, saw and heard nothing out of the ordinary. Afraid Sandy would run off, or find a cat to chase, she called to her, and both of them headed back toward the front door.

On the doorstep she stepped on something sharp. At first Aimee thought she'd cut her foot on a piece of glass, but when she looked down, there was a small, curled shell, not more than three inches long, and in perfect condition. She glanced over her shoulder at the carport area one last time, then followed Sandy through the doorway.

At the last minute, Aimee replaced the shell back on the mat where she'd found it and safely secured them both inside.

CHAPTER 18

ANDY AND SVEN, along with their UN consort, left before nightfall so they could clear a good distance between them and the UNESCO project. It was assumed there was less hostile activity north, especially if they stayed away from the border with Nigeria, and the Niger River, but fingerlings and tributaries formed lakes and smaller rivers throughout the region. It was much faster to navigate these areas in the truck, plus they had the benefit of a heater, which was sometimes a luxury in these parts. Gunnar was a stickler on getting the best equipment possible. All of his four-door trucks were less than a year old, with full on satellite radio and air conditioning too.

Classic maneuvers of some of these militia groups was to raid in one country, and then cross over the border into another where there was no jurisdiction, or where there was less cooperation. There was also the possibility that they'd run into one of these, either fleeing one country or just arriving in another. They would be heavily armed and ruthless, working by their own rules of engagement and more or less autonomous.

Their driver, Adaze, was Nigerian by birth, but his mother was from Benin. Sven had selected him because he seemed to be more friendly than some of the others, plus he was fluent in French. It turned out that he had an uncle he stayed with for several years as a youth in Paris. Sven and Andy could only understand about half of what he said, but he painted quite a picture for them both, chasing girls, getting into small-time trouble, until the family sent him back.

He told them it had always been a dream of his to join the police force, but working for the UN, while perhaps as dangerous, was a better steppingstone for a better life for he and young son. His wife had died after the baby was born, so while on assignment, his son was cared for by his mother's family nearby. He tried to go home as much as possible.

Andy determined he'd been a good pick for two reasons, he seemed genuinely honest about doing good things for his mother's country, and he had good local connections they could rely on.

He told them he was already putting out feelers to some of his family to help the Americans find the hostages. He noted that because the militia group was so hard to find, they obviously had either money to hole up somewhere, or had bought themselves some powerful connections.

"Either way, it smells like money," he said in his heavily accented English, holding his fingers up to his nose. "But they can't hide forever from the *little* people. They can control many, but not all the *little* people."

That confirmed what Andy wanted to believe, that most the population was tired of the carnage and wars. They had never aspired to collecting huge sums of money because it wasn't as valuable as their freedom was. In most cases, the more westernized part of the population had huge appetites for goods from Europe and the U.S. A pair of Nikes would sell for more than a month's salary, but in many portions of the country, it was more a status symbol than having two or three wives.

Sven laughed at that, disagreeing with him. "You should see the Norwegian girls, Adaze, if you had one of them as a wife, you wouldn't say that, my friend."

They had a spirited discussion on the value of women. Andy didn't agree with either one of them but held his tongue.

Adaze lifted the cuff on his pantleg and revealed he wore Nikes. "Gift from Gunnar."

He laughed easily, which was refreshing. "I am going to pass them down to my son."

Andy wondered how many shoes he'd discarded, just thrown away and never bothered to take to the Salvation Army, because it was something he'd have to get in the car and do. One of the best things about his travel was that he'd become very grateful for how he got to live, especially when he compared it to people trying to live and raise families in a war zone.

They were stopped at a police checkpoint, which was the only indication that there had been some militia activity in the area. A European businessman had been killed in a kidnap attempt, Adaze told them. This was information he obtained from the guards. His credentials were an easy ticket through the checkpoint, with an admonishment to be careful, signed off with a peace symbol for benefit of the Americans.

It was an easy cover to say they were American contractors, and most probably believed them, since SEALs didn't normally travel in such small groups. But Sven had been right, having Adaze with them did give them better creds.

As they were driving away from the roadblock, Adaze noticed they had picked up a tail. Someone in a lorry converted to a make-shift camper was following a good distance away.

"Shall I burn some rubber?" he asked, and then gave them a belly laugh.

Before Sven could give permission, he'd floored it,

and left the entire countryside covered in red dust. With only the major highways paved, burning rubber on a dirt thoroughfare was nearly impossible, but he gave it a good try. After they took a fork in the road, they slowed back down to a cruising speed. They were making excellent time and might arrive before it was too dark outside. That was the hope, anyway. They might even beat Tucker and the rest of the crew coming in.

They stopped for a quick bite to eat at a palapa-covered open firepit type kitchen run by a local family their driver knew. Andy tasted some of the hottest chicken he'd ever had, and he wondered how long it might take before his tongue and cheeks would stop throbbing afterwards.

Sven wasn't affected at all. Adaze had dared them to use some of his friend's "special green sauce", but they both declined while he piled it on. Only after he finished did he tell them it worked as a good barrier for fire ants and other pesky bugs.

"Good to know," Sven had said, shaking his head.

This part of the trip was downhill, and they were nearing the outskirts of Kandi, a fairly large city in the province. Instead of arriving from the North, Tucker and the team were arriving direct from France on a chartered flight provided for by Mr. Riley, right into Kandi. Their transport was already taken care of, so

Adaze avoided the main center, and headed up the hill toward their complex.

By foot, this had taken a day, but with the truck, merely five hours.

The first thing Andy remarked was that several of the men stationed at the complex had been pulled off the job. No one was guarding the gate in front, and while nothing appeared out of the ordinary, no one was paying attention like when they'd stayed there before.

He noticed the room he'd set up had been ransacked a bit. He was glad he'd not left any of the expensive medications and equipment, but some of the non-essential medical supplies had been used. Several dirty and bloody bandages remained on the floor. Worst thing about it was that no one knew or would admit to who had done this.

Sven pressed one of the guards Andy recognized from before. "This place was bought and paid for by Uncle Sam. What the hell happened? Where are your men?"

Adaze drifted into the crowd, making like he was looking for some food and water, but he'd promised to listen to what the others were saying in non-English dialogue. Andy figured it wouldn't be safe for him to focus too much on his actions, and just trust the affable UN soldier.

The man with the dark glasses and stoic features was extremely tight-lipped, indicating he understood little of what Sven was asking, which they both knew was only part of the truth. He did look under extreme duress.

"They will be back. Tat's all I can say, Sam." He used the term "Sam" in addressing all the Americans. Andy didn't get that it was used as a sign of disrespect.

While Sven spoke with the guard and two others who had come over to help with this little situation, Andy retreated to the room he'd set up for a treatment and possibly surgery center, if needed. He hoped that Tucker and the rest brought more supplies, because being spread so thin between the two camps was taking a toll on what services he could provide. But it was important to be ready and since this was to be closest to the eventual extraction site, the most necessary.

He'd left a small, locked metal locker the Team sometimes used for storing explosives, and that had now disappeared. It contained vials of antibiotic and a few for pain. Even though it was heavy, Andy now wished he tried somehow to take it along with him. He was good on disinfectant, tape and sterile sutures and still had a dozen bags of saline for emergency hydration. He'd wrapped a set of surgery tools, including a small saw and several scalpels in a baggie, and had wrapped the roll of garbage bags around it so it had remained undetected. He was relieved to find that it was still there.

They heard a truck pull up and Andy saw two young local women, both dressed in scrubs, jump out of the back, pulling large backpacks behind them. Sven knew one of the ladies and helped her with her things.

"Andy! Good news!"

When he rushed outside, Sven was the happiest he'd looked in days.

"Flora and I used to work at the mission in Nigeria back in the day," he had his arm around her chubby shoulder as she put her palm up to her face, embarrassed. "She has the best hands, and demeanor, Andy. I used to call her Florence Nightingale."

"Nice to meet you," Andy nodded to both of them.

Sven walked them over to one of the other rooms that was being used for food storage. Diku, the guard who appeared to be in charge, shouted instructions and soon a couple of folding cots were installed in the cool cinderblock room. A piece of blue plastic tarp was installed over the doorway to give the women privacy.

Andy headed back to the surgery. Sven followed him inside.

"So, what do you think? He asked Sven.

"I'm delighted with the nurses. Not quite sure on the story about the men and vehicles missing, but it could be as he said. They might have been needed elsewhere. We need Adaze's take on things."

"I'm sure he'll be over soon. I agree it was a stroke of genius bringing him along. We want to make sure they don't understand we trust him so, right?"

"My thoughts exactly. So, what's going on with the medical supplies?"

"Lost my antibiotics and some pain killer vials. I still have the pills with me. Still got good surgery tools, disinfectant, saline, but someone came in here and helped themselves to bandages and shit, but nothing we can't live without. I'm sure hoping Tucker will be bringing me more morphine and antibiotics."

"Roger that." Sven scratched his chin. "What are you thinking?"

Andy looked outside, trying to find Adaze. "I want to hear from the driver first, but I'm thinking I should call Peterson and let him know some of these guys went MIA. How did the ladies show up?"

"Diku said someone local asked for them, to help out. Flora is here visiting family and she was conscripted to come up here. She didn't know who ordered it, but the director of her mission in Nigeria knew she was here and sent her over."

The two men stared at each other.

"Which means word has gotten out we're here," Andy muttered to a nodding Sven.

"It does. God, that's what I hate about this place.

You just don't know if they're trying to help you or hurt you. Now, if we had fifty guys, well, we'd get a perimeter set up, you know, go to town. But here, out in the bush, we're on our own."

"Well, we are trying not to become a target."

"Which means they can't arrive too soon. We gotta get the hell out before they're told it's just us."

"Agreed. So, let me know what Adaze says, and I'm going to keep working here. Can you grab me some food?"

"I'll go find him and yes, bring you back something. You got waters?"

"Hell yes."

A few minutes later, Andy had the room straightened and had done a quick clean. He covered surfaces he wanted to stay relatively sterile, knowing he'd have to do it all over again, but it was also a way to track if someone had messed with his stuff. All the garbage was stuffed into a white bag, tied and left outside. He opted not to burn the bloody bandages out of expediency.

Sven brought a paper plate filled with some fried banana-like foods, some local squash, and a skewer of some variety of small fish. A small ball of white rice was set in the middle of the plate for use in eating with his fingers.

"Eat up, then we'll talk," Sven whispered.

All of it, thankfully, was not very spicey and satisfied. It was gone in mere seconds.

"So here's the deal. Word went out about the kidnapping down south. The crew here, when they heard about it, thought it was one of us, and some went to investigate and give assistance. I hate to think the poor bastard lost his life because of us, but he was traveling the same route we were, but we'd stopped, remember? He had a German bodyguard, for all the good it did him, and he had a local driver. The coincidence is stunning, Andy."

"Holy shit. Do you suppose they know about Tucker and them arriving today?"

"Who knows? This crew probably does. Let's hope they get here quick so we can get out before they figure out they got the wrong guy."

"They probably figured it out that a rescue attempt might be made. They were expecting something, right?" Andy asked.

"Maybe. Hard to say. But I'm thinking we need to act fast and then get out of this place. We got one chance. Not like we can hole up for the right time."

"Right."

"I told Adaze to stay with the men and learn everything he can. I'm going to order him around, and warned him about it, not treat him as a friend so he's more useful to us."

"I completely agree. So I need to call Peterson,

then?"

"Yes, do it from the ladies place. No one needs to see you with that SAT phone."

Andy crossed the center of the complex on his way to the ladies' place. He noted that there had been posted guards on the front gate, which pleased him. He gave a casual wave to Diku, more as a show he had confidence whatever had been amiss was now repaired. He got a small nod of the head back in return.

"Flora," he called out to the blue tarp covering their doorway.

"Yes, sir. You can come in, if you like."

Andy pulled the screen back and found the other nurse lying on her back, rubbing her belly. He hadn't noticed before she was several months pregnant. He admired her all the more for working so hard, riding in the back of a truck while in this condition. He gave her a confident smile and a thumbs up, then tapped his belly. She giggled, rolled to her side and covered her face just as Flora had done earlier.

The protector in him rose up, grabbed his heart, and gave it a squeeze. He was in awe that these two willing countrywomen would put themselves and their unborn families in danger to help the mission. It reminded him of the humanity he shared with every peace-loving person around the globe. It was why he did what he did.

A force for good.

"You want something?" Flora asked.

"Did you bring any antibiotics? Mine seemed to walk away while we were on the trail."

"I have a little in my kit, sir, but only a very little. We don't travel with drugs, usually, less dangerous that way."

"I understand. Well, I'm out completely. I'll see if I can get you more when we meet up with our friends."

"Yes, I was told this is an important mission."

"Flora, I'm sure Sven told you we're trying to do this in secret, or as much as possible."

Her smile widened. "I understand, sir, but this is Africa, sir. Even the birds and the trees talk, they whisper. Impossible to do anything in secret here."

Andy was counting on that very thing.

"So you know we're looking for these bad people. You know about the hostages."

"Yes, and I have asked my mother's people for help. Gossip is a big-time interest in my tiny village. Not all the peoples here think you are the enemy. They will be careful, sir."

"Don't do anything stupid, though. Don't risk more than you can afford to. We want you to be safe as well."

"Thank you," she said as she put her hands together in prayer and bowed. "We will do our best. We always do. God is in charge, even though there would be others who think they are." She winked at Adam, leaning in, whispering, "Even though there are those who think otherwise."

"You are Catholic, both of you?" he asked.

"No sir. We are Free Will Baptist. But I work for a Catholic charity. But I don't speak about it and you mustn't either."

Andy was so grateful for a helpful soul he could have hugged her, which would have completely ruined everything.

"So, Flora, I have to make a phone call."

"You want me to leave?"

"No, but I want you to close your ears."

"I understand, sir."

She showed Andy a chair, and then turned, leaned over her co-worker and began whispering, the two of them giggling like two small schoolgirls.

Peterson picked up before it rang.

"Give me a SitRep."

Andy could tell the stress was getting to him.

"We're back at the Kandi base. We've lost some men here, and they got into some of my medical supplies, but it's all fixed now. I'm stripped of antibiotic and pain meds. We're awaiting Tucker and them to arrive. You have any idea when?"

"Shouldn't be too long from now. So your drive

was uneventful? Thank God you're safe. When we heard about the other attempted kidnapping, we feared the worst."

"Kind of a daily occurrence, I'd say. Here's the thing. The guy was a Dutch or Belgian businessman traveling with his German bodyguard, in a small vehicle like we were in, and they had a local driver. Sven and I think the group thought they were us. That's the biggest takeaway and what has us concerned."

"Roger that. I'm going to send this upstairs. They're tracking the phone, so if you lose it, use your regular phone in an emergency. Somehow, you have to get a signal and let us know. And I'm asking for more drones, see if we can follow your group as you head south."

"Right. That's good to know."

"As soon as they arrive, we're taking off. I just don't feel safe here, especially since the area was expecting us. We were followed for a bit at a checkpoint, but our driver lost him, we think."

"Did he work out, then?"

"Couldn't have been more perfect. We're trying to make sure he's not compromised."

"Okay, so let me know when you're on the road. I'll see if I can get some help with the meds up there."

"There are a couple of nurses from Nigeria. Sven

knows one of them. It's great to have them, but did our guys send them?"

"Not that I know of, but I better ask. Can they be trusted to receive the meds?"

"I'd say so, yes. And send a couple protection details for them, too. One of them is pregnant. They're defenseless without any of us around."

"Okay. Let's keep this short. Check back on your departure."

"Thanks, Peterson. See? The plan worked."

"Don't count your chickens just yet, Andy. That's bad luck."

Before Andy could give an answer, Peterson added, "But thanks. I appreciate the support. Just get down here safely. It feels like things are escalating and I'm in agreement, we need to make a move and get out."

He padded Flora's shoulder. "Thanks."

Not halfway across the camp, he heard the sounds of several vehicles approaching. The dust was so heavy he couldn't tell who they were, until he saw the huge, hulking form of Tucker jumping off the back of a small flatbed, carrying a pack that probably weighed as much as he did. On any normal man, the pack would have tipped him on his ass. But this was Tucker.

And Tucker, fresh from becoming a new father, was ready to get back in the fray.

God Bless America!

CHAPTER 19

L AST NIGHT'S EVENT with Sandy's alert, while exactly what she should have done, left Aimee shaken, and she found it difficult to sleep afterwards. Hank Borges' book was no comfort to her. In fact, she couldn't even read any of her favorite go-to romance novels at all. She attempted to watch TV but found no interest in anything. She threw the device at the foot of her bed, and just lay back, staring at the ceiling, giving Sandy a light pet until sleep finally overtook her.

She should have been excited, she thought as she walked outside with the rear seat cover. Still at her toes, the shell lay perfect in its odd placement, a reminder, again, that things were not normal. Everything still seemed to be spinning out of control. The shell incident only underscored that, far from calming her nerves or making her look forward to some communication with Logan, she realized there was a danger that these little gifts were not his work at all, but someone else, messing with her mind.

Dr. Denby, Andy and Shelley were right. Every one of them were right.

She vowed that she'd give the Sheriff's department a visit on the way home.

Sandy watched the passing traffic for a few minutes, then settled down into the seat, her paws outstretched, with her head resting atop them. The dog was quickly becoming the bright spot of her day. She could only imagine how tense she would have been without her companionship. The instant bond she made that day at the shelter was indeed something she could trust and gave her some small sense of protection.

The traffic was massive this morning, so when she arrived at Mr. Kornblum's office, she was a whole ten minutes late. She grabbed the leash and she and Sandy jogged into the large modern building, darting into the third-floor elevator before someone downstairs told her the dog wouldn't be allowed.

Jasper Kornblum's office wasn't as big or expansive as she'd imagined. He had a secretary seated in the tiny lobby and a conference room beyond with a beautiful view of downtown Tampa. There wasn't the buzzing around of associates or customers waiting like she'd seen in some offices. No one offered her an espresso, or a glass of champagne, although today, she could use some alcohol.

Kornblum appeared and was interested in being introduced to Sandy, who gave him her paw.

"Nice pup. She's got a lovely coat, too. How's she with the housebreaking, or did she come already trained?"

"She's good. She's had a run with me. Bought her a dog bed, which I have to return because she prefers to sleep on my bed. So, I guess I'm going to cave on that one, until Andy comes home. He may not be so pleased."

Kornblum had a thick file under his arm, directing her to the conference room. He asked his receptionist to bring a small bowl of water for the dog and two coffees.

"Cream for me. Lots of it," instructed Aimee.

She showed Sandy a sunny corner and had her sit, then took a chair across the polished black conference table from Kornblum. He spread out two files, opening the first and pulling out documents clipped together in several batches, pink arrows affixed to some of the pages.

He lay a single sheet of paper in front of her and turned it around so she could read it.

"These are the very short instructions from Carmen I prepared about six months ago when she was diagnosed as terminal." He slipped another piece of paper beneath it, while Aimee read the verbiage.

It was very short, indicating it was her desire to leave all her worldly goods to Aimee Greer. "But I'm Aimee Carr now."

"The formal legal instructions and the documents you'll sign take that into account. This was her notarized proof of her desire to leave everything to you."

He let her complete the paragraph, and then flipped the page over to reveal a list of items that filled most the page.

"And this is an inventory of what you have inherited."

At first, she focused on the pink arrow at the bottom, but then she began to read. There was a list of four accounts, two with a savings bank and two with a brokerage firm in Sarasota. The total of the stock value, dated today, and bank accounts amounted to over two million dollars.

Her first reaction was to cover her mouth, since her jaw had dropped to nearly touch her chest. Kornblum's amused expression made her think at first, he was playing a cruel trick on her.

"This can't be," she mumbled. "I'm—"

The receptionist brought in two mugs of coffee and lay a glass bowl in front of Sandy, who immediately and very sloppily slurped her way to emptying it.

"I'll get more," the receptionist chuckled.

"I think we're fine, Hailey."

Aimee was in shock and kept reading over the first few lines of assets over and over again, making sure she hadn't misunderstood a decimal point or two.

"She's leaving all this to me? She has no family, no one else she wants to leave money to? I mean, I'm not interfering with some family member's inheritance plans, am I?"

"She had no offspring or siblings. Her parents are gone. Hank left her the house and the bulk of his last twenty-five books sales to her. And, she had some success on her own. Quite a bit of success. She was a shrewd investor, lived a very simple life, and saved like there was no tomorrow. I think in many ways, she was a lot like you, Aimee. Her needs were small, and she really didn't enjoy spending money. She liked saving it."

"I thought maybe when you told me, that perhaps we could get a new car or pay for some of the construction we've been saving for to complete on the house, but this—this is nowhere near what I thought it could be. I don't know what to say."

"Say thank you. Say it to her."

Aimee teared up immediately. Kornblum slid the tissues over to her and waited, his hands folded in front of him. Sandy had been alerted to Aimee's tears and walked over to sit next to her. It made her laugh that the dog had already developed the sense that she was emotional.

"So, how does this work, then?"

"Well, I have several papers you will need to sign, and we'll have Hailey notarize. You'll want to meet with the bank representatives so they can explain what has to happen on their end, their paperwork. You'll be given access to her jewelry in a safe deposit box. The contents are listed here." He tapped a list of contents, which included two gold bands, two cocktail rings, a tennis bracelet, and a child's heart-shaped locket.

"What's this?"

"Apparently, there's a letter of explanation in the box. I wasn't given any information about it."

"But did she have a daughter?"

"No, she's signed affidavits that she had no children of her own. That's stipulated in the will and all the estate documents. I'm afraid that mystery you're going to have to work out on your own."

"I don't know what to do." Aimee was wondering how Andy would take the news and wondering if she should wait to tell him after he got home. She didn't want to distract him from the importance of his mission.

"Why don't we start by signing the paperwork. Then I can file the proper notices and give you authorization to have access. It will take about thirty days to complete everything, but after that time, you'll be able to access everything and do what you like with it. I do suggest you meet with the managers and the portfolio managers at the two brokerage houses. I usually tell people to just leave things where they are at, until you decide what your plans are for the money. They can help you strategize an exit plan, if you need it. This is also a good time to interview them and figure out for yourself whom you want to continue working with. Maybe wait until Andy returns, but you're not required to. This is your money, Aimee. She knew about your wedding plans, but it's your sole separate property."

"I wouldn't think of doing anything without Andy's input."

"Of course, I would be the same way, Aimee."

"Do I have to decide anything now?"

"Well, you can decide to refuse the money. You can do that. But all we need today is your signature." He handed her a pen. "And tell you face to smile. Trust me, this is a good thing. She'd want to see you happy."

Suddenly an idea popped into her head. "Her funeral? Can I pay for her funeral?"

"No, that's already been taken care of. It wasn't anticipated there would be many in attendance, so she prepaid for a small service and asked that her ashes be spread at the beach. I can have them released to you, if you like."

The idea of sprinkling the contents of Carmen's life into the bay filled her with sadness. "I couldn't—" she broke down in tears again, resting her head on her forearms. Kornblum grabbed one of her hands and squeezed.

"It's going to take time to get used to this. This is a gift, Aimee. Nothing you need to feel guilty of, or sad about. It was her way of celebrating her life by sharing it with you, you and Andy, and whomever else you want to. In time, that's the way you'll see it, I'm sure."

"When? When is the funeral?"

"In three days."

"I want to go," she mumbled, wiping the streaks of tears from her cheeks with his Kleenex.

"I'll be there too. I'm bringing my wife as well. I think we'll be the only ones, but you never know."

"Can we wait for Andy?"

"No. But you can have another service, if you like. Maybe he could help you spread the ashes. I think he'd want to help you with that."

He was right, of course. She stared at the pen, still clutched in her fingers, and began to look for pages with pink arrows at the bottom.

She'd been right all along. That house at Sunset Beach was magic. Everything that flowed from it was magic. Her life had been forever altered the day she found it and fell in love with it, and the man who gave her the confidence to go after it. What if Andy had said no? What if her mother hadn't left her the money to purchase it? What if she'd decided it was too old and in too much need of repair and should be torn down? What if she had never come to the Florida Gulf Coast and walked the beach? That's where her life had begun. That's when it all started.

Magic. Pure magic!

CHAPTER 20

S VEN WAS THE first on the team to greet Tucker. The two men had an extreme bear hug. Tucker towered over Sven by several inches and was probably double his body size, but it made no difference, Sven tried to pick him up anyway.

They'd arrived in brand new white four-door pickups, which left room in the back for backpacks and equipment. Tucker had ridden there with the equipment. Kelly Fieldling made her way out of the passenger's seat of the first truck. Fredo, Danny Begay, Armando, T.J. Talbot, Jake Green all exited the second vehicle. T.J. and Danny approached Andy.

"How's it going, kid?" T.J. was grinning, carrying a large backpack with a red cross on it. "I understand from the Headshed that you are short on antibiotics. I got y'all fixed up kid, and some painkillers too." He shoved the backpack into Andy's belly.

"Cool." Andy slipped the pack over his shoulder.

"Okay, I got mine. Where's all the rest for you guys?"

Fredo punched him in the arm. "Nice one, bro. You holding up okay?"

"Of course. Got good mentors," Andy answered.

The new team members were still getting unloaded. They had brought along two extra guards, plus the drivers. Diku greeted the Africacorps troops warmly, as did several of the compound guards under his command.

Their temporary meet and greet was halted as Sven drew the SEALs into a circle and explained their dire situation.

"Look, guys. I'm not going to sugarcoat it at all. We're in kind of a shitstorm here. I'm sure you know that Peterson and the rest of the team, Andy's team, are holed up down south with the UNESCO project and Gunner Larssen's men. They're okay, but probably not very secure. That's why you guys are here."

Tucker was the first to respond. "Just lay it out, Sven. Please just tell us what you want us to do and we're here for you."

"Well, Andy and I have come back here to double check the compound, and it appears that the site partially abandoned, and some of the medical was used by unknowns. We really aren't sure—still trying to figure that out. These guys have worked pretty hard," he pointed to Diku, who was having his own private conversation with his colleagues.

"I think they're honest, and half this team headed south to investigate the kidnapping of the European businessman, and I guess everyone here thought it was us. We need to get south quickly before they figure out they got the wrong guys, and if the whole area thinks that one of us on this ambushed team was murdered by this militia group, then good for us. But they won't take long to figure out who they really got. We need to get to safety and to Peterson and his group, before they get cut off. We think the militia group that murdered the businessman is the same group that has the hostages."

"Good on you, Andy. You guys risked your butts to get up here," T.J. barked.

"So, you're saying we got to get out of Dodge then. Is that right?" asked Fredo.

"That's what we're saying Fredo." Andy was sure everyone got the message.

"So how do we do this? You got any thoughts on whose trucks we take and when we leave?" asked Tucker.

Andy stepped forward and answered him, "I think we need three trucks, we got two, we may need one of yours. Or we can take a third here. But we got to go right away. As in *now*."

"Okay then, so no need to unload." Armando set

his bag down and headed back to the truck.

"T.J., you and I need to meet with a couple of nurses who showed up this afternoon. I want to make sure they've got some meds for our return trip. And I need to give them instructions. So, let's go on up there and then we'll all meet you back here, but get ready to roll out of here like in 10 minutes, okay?"

The team was used to these sorts of excursions where they had little time to decompress, rest up or refresh themselves after a long flight and trip over. But this is what it was all about. And if it was urgent, it was urgent.

On the way across the courtyard to the nurses' room, Andy whispered to T.J., "Truth is T.J., I got to call Peterson, and I need to do it where no one will see me. What you can do is introduce yourself to the nurses, have Flora and her assistant meet you in the surgery center we set up, and you can unload some of your vials of antibiotics and maybe three or four pain meds, some morphine, whatever you brought."

"Sure thing. How did these ladies show up?"

"You know, T.J., this is Africa. I have no fucking clue who sent them, but they were sent by someone in the Archdiocese in Nigeria. They work for a Catholic charities group. Their coordinator over there is a Frenchman, we don't have any contact with him, but Sven knows Flora, and he trusts her. So, the bottom line is someone knows we might need medical assistance, which is a whole other problem."

"I got ya. So, they're staying here?"

"Yeah, unfortunately. I can't really take these women into combat. They're not trained, and I'd be afraid we'd spend a lot of resources protecting them. But we have a couple of extra guards on their way over, or at least I requested it, to protect them. We're going to take some of these guys, but we have to leave some behind obviously to man the compound. This will be where we come back to after our mission, and then we'll head up north to get the transport out of Niger. But somebody's got to stay here and protect the camp site, and the nurses. And I need a little bit of medical supplies here, just for giggles."

"Giggles?"

"God T.J., I'm running out of words here. It's just a big clusterfuck. But we're doing the best we can."

"I'd say, my man, you're doing pretty damn good."

He knocked on the outside of the building and called through the blue plastic sheet to the nurses. Flora pulled aside the screen and invited them in.

"Flora, this is T.J. Talbot, he's a medic from Team 3, and I've served with him. He's going to take you over to the surgery and help restock some antibiotics and a little bit of other stuff too, so you tell him what you think we are going to need. Okay?"

"Sure thing, Andy." She looked up at the tall medic and curtsied in front of him, which Andy thought was funny. T.J. tried to cover his smile with his hand, but both ladies were embarrassed and giggled like school-girls.

"Nice to meet you." Flora pushed her assistant in front who also curtsied and greeted T.J. with a very soft handshake.

The two nurses left, and T.J. followed behind carry-ing the medic pack. Andy retrieved his sat phone and dialed Peterson.

"Tell me they got there safely, Andy." Peterson barked.

"Yes sir, they did. We didn't get any of Collin's guys, but we got seven, including Kelly Fieldling. We got Fredo and Danny, we got Armando, of course Tucker, and we have T.J. and Jake Green as well, so we got a good group. I'm grateful for the medical supplies that T.J. brought."

"That's good. I'm glad they got that together. So, when are you leaving?"

"We're going to go now, even though it's dark. Any intel to say that the roads are not passable or there's some kind of hazard ahead?" Andy asked.

"We're going to have you traced, and we will notify you if we find any activity. It's easier for us to track at night, so although it's going to be more dangerous for you, I'd prefer it. But be careful. And you got local drivers there, so hopefully they can get around anything that should come up. I'll make sure the guys who have the eyes in the sky give us a major heads up in case something forms.

"Thanks, Peterson. One thing I didn't mention before was that several of the drivers have family in the area and the word has gone out to them to bring back any local intel. Several of them have told us that there doesn't appear to be anything going on here, so we think they're either headed your direction or they're even further south than you. But I hope we don't run into anybody, and if so, you know we'll deal."

"Okay then, so I'm going to assume you're on the road in like less than 10, right?"

"You would be correct. We'll see you in about five, six hours?"

"No, I think it will be closer to sunrise. But you stay safe, hear?"

"Absolutely."

Andy left the storage room and headed over to the surgery where T.J. was still instructing Flora on several items that he brought for her. He stashed a few things in bins that were mislabeled, to throw off anybody who might be looking for antibiotics or the pain meds, and they all agreed that most of the supplies needed to be taken on the road, since they had nearly 25 men to take care of. Andy told Flora that two guards were on their way over to give them extra protection, and then there would be at least five remaining behind to man the complex. He told her it would be okay to do minor triage and first aid for any of the men in the compound, but not to encourage locals to come in and seek medical attention, as might happen.

"Just tell them you're a privately contracted clinic, if you have to say anything," he added.

Andy and T.J. approached the trucks again. Sven had coordinated who was going to stay behind in the complex, and who was going to go with the group. Diku wanted to go, and he promised his second-in-command would take good care of the nurses and guard the complex. With some hesitation, Sven agreed after checking with Andy.

"I just want to make it so that they have enough protection for now, and I hope this guy isn't going to leave. Diku, we can't have this place abandoned while we're gone, I trust that if you stayed, that wouldn't happen. I'm going to be really pissed if these guys abandon their post."

Diku shook his head. "No, man. They good. They good men."

Sven pulled Andy aside. "I think they can be paid a little something, what do you think?" he whispered.

"You mean Kelly brought it?"

Sven nodded.

"Then I'd say yeah. Give them something. I'm sure it doesn't have to be much."

Sven brought Kelly over and the three of them discussed payment.

"Here's what I propose," Kelly said. "I got hundred-dollar packets, and five-hundred-dollar packets. I'd like to give the guards that stay a hundred-dollar packet. I think that's good money to them."

"Hell yeah," Sven said.

"I think that's half a year's salary," said Andy.

"So, I'm going to recommend giving a fiver to Diku, and tell him he'll get a bonus when the mission is successfully rendezvoused with the other team? You okay with that?"

"Absolutely." said Andy. Sven nodded. "Another five hundred to Sven for Adaze, too."

"Completely agree," said Sven.

"Okay then, give me two minutes with Diku, and I'll make sure he gets his men paid."

Two vehicles were loaded from the compound. One was the four-door pickup that they had arrived in, and one was a delivery van that would seat several more and carry most of their equipment. It was decided that the vehicles picking up the team at the airport would return.

With several guards left behind, that left five to accompany the team, and although it was a little light, Andy was grateful that with two men they could communicate with, Diku, and their driver, the others were just for extra firepower, should it be needed. It also added more legitimacy, since they were traveling in UNESCO trucks, and if there was not a local contingent, somebody along the way would notice.

They began their journey just before the stroke of midnight. Before they left, Diku had his man distribute water, and a small package of sweet potatoes, chicken, and leafy green vegetables of some kind, wrapped in a rice ball. It didn't taste great, but Andy was grateful for the nourishment. The water was heavenly.

With any luck, they'd be meeting up with Peterson and his team, before morning.

CHAPTER 21

AIMEE DECIDED TO drop by Shelley's school, and found her car in the parking lot, so took Sandy and knocked on her classroom door. She could hear Latin jazz music playing loudly in the room, so when no one answered, she knocked a little harder.

Shelley's unmade up face was quite the sight. She had a red bandana around her head, cutoff jeans, and a halter top t-shirt. Aimee laughed when she thought Shelley did not quite have the appearance of a respectable schoolteacher.

"Just wanted to introduce you to Sandy."

Shelley kneeled and eyed Sandy's face straight on. "What a beautiful puppy. She's a girl?"

"Well, she's not a puppy, she's full grown, and she's spayed. It's Sandy. Sandy meet Shelley."

Sandy put her paw on Shelley's knee as if understanding the formal introduction.

"Aw, you are such a good girl. You're going to keep

my friend Aimee safe? Is that right?"

The dog's ears went into alert, and then she looked up at Aimee.

Shelley stood, arching her back, with her hands on her hips. "So, I don't think you've seen my classroom this year. I'm right in the middle of preparing a module on the oceans, which is the study they're going to do for the next three months. You see?"

She pointed to a wall that was filled with cut out pictures of fish, looking like a huge kelp forest window with various sea creatures big and small. A list of vocabulary terms was listed on the side. It was a colorful display of Shelley's creative abilities.

"We do this so that by the time the whales start moving, the kids will have some context. Most of the kids around here know quite a bit about sea life, because they live here. But many of them don't know about the migrations and why they happen, and it's I think my favorite module." She examined her handiwork, turned to Aimee and smiled.

"That's fantastic Shelley," Aimee said. She was really a talented teacher, Aimee thought, and wondered what it would have been like to have a teacher like her growing up.

"So, we got the introduction out of the way, what are you really here for? Have you heard from Andy?" Shelley's direct questions shouldn't have been a surprise to Aimee by now, but they still caught her off guard.

"You promised you weren't going to ask me that again."

"You're right. I'm sorry." Shelley put both hands up in the air and shook her head. "I forget, and I know you'll forgive me."

"Of course. But I do have some other news, and I would be bursting to tell Andy, but I'll just have to do it when he calls me. I got a call yesterday that Carmen Hernandez passed away suddenly. The attorney asked me to come into his office this morning to go over some paperwork. And it turns out she has left me some money."

Shelley stared at her, her eyes getting wide. "How *much* money?"

Aimee rocked her head from side to side, fidgeting with what she should tell her. "A lot. I mean, Shelley, it's a lot."

"Oh my gosh!"

"I don't want you to breathe a word about this with anybody. I don't want a soul to know, for obvious reasons."

"Done!" Shelley said, crossing her heart.

"It gives Andy and I some flexibility, in what we do with the house, and other things too."

"I'd say so. Then, why aren't you like jumping for

joy?"

"Because I just don't feel this money is mine. I mean, I didn't earn it. I'm not a relative of hers. I only got to meet her one time."

"What do you mean? It's what she wanted to do, Aimee."

"It just doesn't feel right yet. I don't understand why she chose me. It's like one of those things you always hear growing up, *if it's too good to be true it is.* I just somehow can't fathom that it's real. I mean, this will change our lives for the remainder of the time we're here. I can do things that I never thought I could do before. And it opens up a whole set of choices, that I just—Now I've got all these decisions I have to make."

"You *have to* make?" Shelley asked with a scowl.

"No, it's just that I want to be a good steward of it."

"Oh, for Christ's sakes Aimee, enjoy it. I think she gave you the money because you fell in love with her place, you were perhaps the daughter she never had. I think she wanted you and Andy to be happy. It made her happy knowing that. I wouldn't question it any further. I would enjoy it. Why can't you just do that Aimee?"

"I guess because I feel like I don't deserve it."

"Listen to yourself, Aimee. Just listen to what you're saying. That's nonsense. You have to embrace it and accept it and live your life to the fullest. You're given an opportunity, to do something that like you said others can't do. So, this is your chance. I mean in a way, it's kind of your new job, right?"

Aimee thought about it for a minute and understood the logic. "It just hasn't sunk home yet."

Shelley grabbed her and gave Aimee a bear hug. "You are such a big doofus, Aimee. I think you're one of the most honest, wonderful and loving people I've ever met in my entire life. I can't wait to see what you do with that money. *You deserve it.*"

Armed with that bit of encouragement from Shelley, Aimee took Sandy to the dog park on the way home. She stared down at her cell phone, wishing she could get a call from Andy. She had not remembered being so anxious last time he was on deployment, but that was before they got married. She wondered why that would change, and then she started to think about all the other changes that had occurred in her life.

The money was certainly something that was occupying her mind, but Logan, and his reaching out to her, was also an issue.

And it all came at the same time when she was worried for Andy's mission and safe return. She decided to just accept what was here today, and have faith that Andy would call her soon, and try to focus on some of the things she might want to accomplish with her new inheritance.

They arrived home, and Aimee fixed Sandy her dinner early. She sat in front of the TV with the dog at her side, eating a rice bowl. She was going to turn in early and watched the weather report which indicated there was going to be a huge storm arriving in the evening. Outside, she repositioned the chairs and secured a table, and made sure that the umbrellas were tucked to the side of the house so that any wind that would accompany the storm wouldn't damage them.

She checked all the doors and windows, making sure they were properly closed and locked, brought her dishes into the kitchen, then took Sandy upstairs so she could read in bed. As she continued with Hank's story, the wind started howling, Sandy's ears peaking at the sound of thunder and lightning. It was going to be a wild night, she thought. But she was used to them now, even though this was an unusually late storm.

Out of her bedroom window, she could see white caps in the bay already, and hear the fronds of trees slapping against the side of the house and the wet road from Gulf Boulevard as traffic brought people home.

She turned off the light and decided to turn in. Again, she stared at the ceiling. She thought about the magic of the house. She thought about her future, filled with possibilities. And drifted then off to sleep.

It was sometime late in the evening when Sandy started to bark again, startling her. She slipped on her robe and followed the dog downstairs. The dog headed straight for the front door.

"Sandy, is someone there?" Then, she yelled through the door, "If you're out there, I can't talk to you. You can't come by. You have to leave me alone. Please stop."

She listened for a sign, but with the howling of the wind and weather outside, she did not want to open the door. She didn't turn on any of the lights and moved to the kitchen window to see if she could detect anyone outside the front door area, but the area appeared clear. Sandy wanted to go out, but Aimee discouraged her. "I'll take you in a few hours, in the morning. When it's not so miserable and dark outside."

Just then, several thunderous roars shook the whole house. It felt as if lightning had struck right there right in front of her or perhaps right on the beach as she'd seen from time to time. She stared out the sliding glass door and all she could see were raindrops flowing horizontally. Sandy ran over to the sliding glass door as another huge bolt of lightning went off. Aimee could see in that flash of light the figure of a man, leaning into the window. She jumped back, calling for Sandy. Another bolt of lightning illuminated the patio, and the area was clear.

Had she imagined this? Was there really somebody

out there? Or was it just her mind playing tricks on her?

She looked at the cell phone in her hand and decided she needed to give Shelley a call first and then corrected herself and called the Pinellas County Sherrill's Office.

The clerk who answered the phone was made aware of the fact that there had been an incident report on file, and Aimee asked her to look it up so she could give further detail. She asked if it would be possible for an officer to come over and check the grounds, making sure that Logan or whoever the person was wasn't still in the area. She told the clerk that she feared for her life.

The dispatcher agreed to send someone over.

In less than ten minutes, two flashing police cars drove up through her carport. She opened the door and let them inside. Both of them were dressed in yellow rain slickers, water dribbling down their faces.

"Mrs. Greer?"

"Yes, I'm the one who called."

"You reported a suspicious person?"

"Yes, I did. Please, come in." She handed them a tea towel for their hands and face.

"Thanks, ma'am. Much appreciated. So, tell me what he looked like."

"He was wearing a hoodie that looked like it was

soaking wet and he was tall, thin. He could be my brother. The last time I saw him close was many years ago, but I think I've had a sighting since and this person looked like the man I saw in the parking lot a year ago. Maybe he wanted to come inside and get out of the rain, and—"

"No ma'am. If he's leaning up next to the window, that's breaking the law. Especially in the middle of the night. You were right to call us."

"So, you'll do a search and then come back and let me know what you find?"

"Yes ma'am, just give us a few minutes, and we'll be right back."

The two officers left their lights flashing as they began searching the area with flashlights. Aimee closed the front door. Sandy sat at her side.

The storm continued to rage, with intermittent thunder and lightning, which made her jump every time she heard it. Sandy's head was whipping from side to side checking the front door and then the back sliding glass door at every thunderous noise. "That's a good girl. This will all be over soon, I hope. The good guys are here Sandy."

Several minutes later, she heard another knock at the door and opened to the two officers.

"Ma'am, we haven't found anything, but it looks like you have some footprints on your patio and perhaps some prints on the sliding glass door. It's probably not too much we can do tonight. But I'm going to recommend that we keep a patrol car here for the night just cruising back and forth on the street and throughout the neighborhoods. That would probably make you feel a little more secure, right?"

"Oh absolutely. Thank you so much, officer."

A squawking noise came over a little loudspeaker affixed to the officer's chest. He answered the call and stepped to the side to have a private conversation with a dispatcher.

When he returned, he addressed her, "It appears that you have some neighbors nearby, who report a break-in. They're outside. Mind if I let them in to talk?"

"Absolutely."

The officer opened the door and a middle-aged couple emerged, in their pajamas, with rain slickers on and boots.

The woman started first, "We live just four houses up. We came back to Florida this afternoon. We've had the place rented, and everything was cleaned for us after the last tenant. But when we got here, and we walked in it looked like somebody had been living in the house. We found a side door unlocked, but nothing's really damaged or anything."

"Why do you say someone's been living there?"

"Well, they left a backpack and an old smelly sleeping bag in the living room. So, when I saw the flashing lights and saw the activity over here, we just thought we should come over and tell you. We were going to go down to the police department in the morning and report it."

"How long has it been vacant?"

She looked up at her partner, who answered, "It's been three and a half weeks, almost four weeks."

"Other than the sleeping bag and backpack, how could you tell that somebody had been living there?" the officer asked.

"Because whomever it was broke into our owner pantry, which we hadn't unlocked yet. We had a bunch of items stored for us; granola bars, Gatorade, waters, things like that. It looks like whomever has been living there has been living off the juice and waters and snacks in the owner closet. There wasn't anything in the refrigerator and he didn't touch anything else, except he left a mess on the kitchen.

"Food and things? What kind of mess?"

"Some kind of a project. He got out one of our toolboxes and had pliers and things all over the table with shells and crap."

Aimee ran to the kitchen counter and picked up the charm bracelet that had been left for her. "Did it look like this? Like some of these things?"

"Exactly. So that's what he was doing. There was wire and shells and all kinds of garbage—you know, stuff you find on the beach. It looked like he was making something. Something exactly like that."

Several minutes later, the neighbors left after exchanging phone numbers with Aimee They invited her to call them anytime if she had anymore sightings. Everyone was happy that there would be a patrol car out front, which might deter anybody who was still in the area. The neighbors left. Aimee needed to add one more bit of information for the report.

"I need to give you the phone number for Dr. Denby. It's already in the report, but I want to be sure you have it in case he shows up tonight. If this is indeed my brother Logan, Dr. Denby treated him at his center in Sarasota. I think he would be agreeable to taking him back, if you find him. Maybe take him directly there, instead of jail or wherever you put these guys."

"Well, that's a problem. Because breaking and entering is against the law. It's a misdemeanor unless something major was stolen or broken. But it's still against the law, and we aren't allowed to just pick someone up and then release them to a nonsecure facility. More than likely he'd have to be held overnight. But I can certainly put that in the file and if we do apprehend him this evening on our shift, I can make sure that message gets to them. You might want to alert your doctor friend to what's happened here. I assume he knows that you've had some contact with him?"

"Yes, he knows all about it. He suggested his name be given out."

"Then I would give him a call and let him know. Who knows, maybe he'll show himself. It's hard to say with these guys, though. Especially with the long history of drug and alcohol abuse. You know they aren't thinking straight. And you're right to not let him into your home. You do have to treat him like a threat. And now he's not only a threat to you, but he's a threat to other people and their property as well, and that's the real problem. When they start spiraling out of control, then they become a danger to not only themselves but everybody around them. So please do not have any contact with him if he tries to approach you."

It was going to be another one of those nights, where she would be tossing, listening to the thunder and lightning, seeing the flashing lights glow through her windows, and thinking about being on the edge, between Aimee's old life, and her new life. She wished Andy would call.

There was just no getting around it, she needed to talk to her husband.

CHAPTER 22

THE TWO TRUCKS barreled down the roadway, wound through parts of the outer city of Kandi, and back out into the stretches of highway headed to the lake region. They crossed over numerous bridges that were not guarded, which was one of the advantages of traveling at night. Andy made a quick call to make sure that the tracing birds were up and following him and got confirmation from Peterson that yes, indeed, they were being watched.

Diku and Adaze were the perfect drivers for this type of excursion, because both had spent time in Benin, and had family currently living in several of the nearby villages. So, if a road was washed out, they knew all the back ways to get around it. In fact, Andy figured they might even have a leg up on some of the militiamen who came over the Nigerian border.

All along the way, they kept their eyes peeled for lorries with troop transport, or large bands of militia.

The little villages they crossed through and around were quiet, very little lighting, mostly bonfires occasionally seen out in the fields. Some field hands did do work at night, processing and boxing, nearly everything was shut down at dark.

The roads were so full of ruts, and the diesel motors so loud, that conversation was limited. Andy and several others took the time to catch a few Zs. He had been on the road for two days straight, with very little sleep.

About an hour into the trip, Andy's sat phone pinged.

"We got a sighting of maybe twenty to thirty men, who've just flown in from a remote village in Nigeria, arriving in a couple of birds of unknown origin. If you could try to swing by and snap some photographs, we're going to see if anybody is headed your way. Norfolk wants to have eyes on the ground."

"Roger that." Andy gave the instructions about the group and Adaze maneuvered around some of the back alleyways of a small town, knowing a facility in that area that could house helicopters and possibly drop and store troops. It was an old hangar that had been used for farming operations, crop dusting and delivery of materials, but the military often used it in the past. The militias did as well. They parked in front of an abandoned school yard, anxious to get in the middle of the fray.

Sven suggested that Andy and the others stay in the trucks with the drivers while he take Tucker and TJ, Fredo and a two other SEALs to investigate, hopefully get pictures for the men upstairs. They disappeared into the night without making a sound, as if the blackness swallowed them whole.

Roughly 15 minutes later, the group returned, wasting no time to get back on the road. Sven took to uploading some of their photos, and Andy verified with Peterson afterward that they'd been received.

"I'll get you back a report," Peterson barked. "Your assessment of the group?"

Sven leaned over and spoke into the phone, "Sir, they look like recruits of some kind, but they're bedded down for the night in a bunker nearby. And I don't see any trucks nearby, so they're not going anywhere, at least not tonight. It could be that they're getting ready for some kind of an operation, or exercise, but they look private like possibly guards for some Benin military operation, but the uniforms are non-descript, so I don't know for sure, but they don't look like militia. And with the militia, you'd see the trucks with the .50s on the back, and I just don't see it. I see nothing but passenger vehicles over there."

"Okay then, carry on. Get yourself south, and we'll check in later when we have some results for you."

About forty minutes later, Peterson pinged again.

"We got a road closure up ahead. It's a regular full-on blockade. You want to avoid it, no option. They tell me there's lots of troops and trucks, and it doesn't look good."

"Will do." Andy thought about the pictures, "Hey, Peterson, they say anything about the pix?"

"Negative. No interest."

After he disconnected, Adaze indicated he knew a long way around the checkpoint that would carry them in a wide loop but would probably delay their return a good half hour.

"We may have to go through some rice fields. Maybe we go through fingerlings," Adaze said. "But I think it is the safest way. We won't get stuck with these brand-new trucks, and we'll avoid the road closure. Something must have happened to cause all this interest at this time of night."

Sven looked at TJ and Tucker, all of them nodding to themselves. It was obvious something had happened back there, but without firsthand information and without being directed to inquire further, they were happy to avoid it.

Andy thought the truck was going to tilt on its side as they headed off a small embankment and through a tiny rivulet. The heavy vehicle came up the other side and almost hit a water buffalo standing right there, the headlights blinding him temporarily. Adaze was quick to maneuver around the beast. "You don't want to hit one of those. They got friends, and they come after you, I've seen them chase a truck for 10 kilometers." He laughed but the rest of the team was quiet.

It took several bumpy roads before they returned to the wide red highway headed straight south to Benot. The road wasn't paved, but it had been frequently used and had been rocked on several occasions. The potholes were minimum, and the closer they got to the city, the faster they were able to travel. The road widened slightly and allowed for a second lane of travel.

It was an easy stretch to get back. They arrived at Benot, through the town center and passed by several of the downtown offices and buildings they had been scoping the day before.

The sun had just started sending rose-colored shards of light into the sky, which highlighted soaring purple and gray thunder clouds, threatening a storm they said was on the way.

When they pulled up to the compound, the UNESCO site, Andy was surprised at the quantity of work that had been completed by the men left behind. They had constructed a whole lodge house which could serve as a dining hall, meeting hall/bunkhouse, filled in the walls with a small forest of cut pine logs. They had built corrals and pens and had managed to build a block latrine and storage unit, with massive wooden doors that could be locked and secured, a perfect place to store their ammunition, supplies, or things they didn't want animals and other curious villagers to get into.

Gunnar came running out of one of the little cabins, holding a lantern. He had a smile that extended nearly from ear to ear.

"My friends, my friends, welcome, welcome to the sanctuary!"

Peterson appeared out of the dark and made the introductions, ordering the men to take up shelter in various cabins that Gunnar provided for them. Another cabin was assigned to Diku, Adaze and the other Africacorps men.

Peterson called for a meeting in the lodge building in 10 minutes.

Kit, Connor and Dallas greeted the new men from Team 3. After everyone took seats, several brought over local dishes that had been prepared, heating them with microwaves and sending them down the communal table. While they munched on finger food, Peterson, took the floor. He pinned a map to the wall and began discussions about hotspots in several regions, indicating where there had been some recent sightings of interest.

"We have two locations that we're most curious about. One of them is actually an old gentleman's club that had been set up during the European days. It had been owned until recently by a very eccentric Dutch businessman, who maintained a quasi-brothel there. However, he's gone, and it appears either relatives or someone he sold the property to is now running it. If they're hold up there, then the hostages are probably not going to be in terrible condition, because the buildings and the grounds have been well maintained, and it won't be like sleeping out in the bush. It could also explain why we haven't seen these people because they're staying put. It is usually well fortified and guarded."

"The other place we're looking at is a school that was in session until recently. The local leaders had had problems with kidnappings and children missing, so they closed the school for the rest of the year. There are several classrooms, offices and a large auditorium, and any one of those facilities could also hold a number of hostages, as well as house militia men."

"How many men are at each of these locations, do the drones tell us that?" Tucker wanted to know.

"We have multiple sightings at the school, however, right now not many at the villa. So, our decision was to check out the school first, and see who's there. It could be that they are using both spaces, but probably not."

Fredo asked if it was determined that the girls from the school in Benot were also being housed here.

"You mean held with the other hostages? I'd say that's affirmative, if you ask me," answered Sven.

Peterson agreed with him as did several others.

"With the sun up, we don't have the luxury of the drones. But there was no major force headed this direction, so we're thinking we'd give you guys a few hours to rest up, get some grub, shower, get your gear in order, and we check out as soon as it becomes dark. Kelly, you and Gunnar and Sven need to have a conversation and get some of these men paid. Gunnar is expecting a very generous pay day, and we'd like to keep them being so cooperative."

The team laughed.

"I know what he likes, and I brought lots of it," said Kelly.

Peterson turned to Sven, whispering, "I know you've been awake more than you've been asleep Sven, but I do think we need to meet with Mr. Sabi, get a temperature read. Are you going to be able to go in with me and Kelly and maybe take one of the drivers, and pay him a visit?"

"Maybe we take Doctor Carr as well?"

"Sure, the more the merrier I guess."

Andy was not delighted with this. He was hoping to have a date with his bed. He looked up at Peterson and held a pretend phone to his ear raising his eyebrows. Peterson gave him a thumbs up which meant Andy was going to have the opportunity to call his wife when they got to town.

Andy took a quick shower and grabbed some food. He left his medic bag with TJ and, armed with his SIG Sauer and two knives as well as several chloroform packets, he was ready to go. All five of them piled into the truck and Adaze headed toward town.

"So what's the deal with this guy, who is he really and who owns him?" Kelly asked.

Sven smiled back at her, gave her a wink and said, "Oh, he's probably owned by some woman, who leads them around by the nose. Isn't that the way all powerful men are handled?"

"You've got that right, Sven. I can see you've learned some things with your time in the bush." Kelly followed up that comment with a glare.

"Oh, but it would have been so much more fun if you'd been here."

She smiled in return. "I mean it. Who is he really and who does he work for?"

Peterson filled her in on their conversation with Sabi before. "We're thinking that not much goes on in the way of security and operations that he doesn't know about. Maybe he works both ends, and he owes his loyalties to the highest bidder. So, if there are church or missions that need help or assistance, they pay for guards that he hires out through the local police and fire department. But if somebody else comes along and pays more, then they get more guards or the guards for the other group are bought off and disappear."

"Kelly, we didn't get too far the last time we were here. I walked away with a sheaf of paperwork, which I've left back at the camp. He's a big one on paperwork," Andy added.

"Oh, they usually are."

Kelly was flirting with Sven very overtly. It made Andy feel a little uncomfortable.

"So, we're going to ask him for permission to open up the clinic, right?" she asked.

"Yes," said Peterson. "And we're going to ask about location and see what he gives us. And then we're going to ask him some questions about the recent kidnappings and find out what his take is on them. What I'd like to see is if we can determine he had anything to do with them, and I think we need to come to it from the point of being concerned about our safety like, is this a safe area?"

Kelly nodded her head in agreement.

They parked in the nearly vacant parking lot of the Ministry Building, leaving Adaze alone in the truck. The delightful lobby was air conditioned like a refrigerator. A guard directed them to the Commissioner of Health's office. This time, the door was closed. Walking inside, they asked for Sabi. The young receptionist placed her hand over the receiver and asked them what they wanted.

"We're here to see Mr. Sabi, we are the Americans who came by to see him last week?" Peterson said.

"Just a moment. I will see if he's available." She hung up her call.

She slipped into Mr. Sabi's private office closing the door behind her. After some discussion, she reappeared. "He will see you now."

Since Adaze was staying at the truck, the four of them again entered the office with only one chair. He offered it to them just like before. "Please, gentlemen, take a seat."

His eyes danced with delight, watching the men scramble make a decision who had the seniority to sit in the chair. That was Peterson. Mr. Sabi eyed Kelly suspiciously as she began to speak.

"Mr. Sabi, my name is Kelly Fieldling, and I work for the State Department." She pulled out her badge, and the Commissioner nodded with respect, sitting more upright. "So, this is not private then, this is for my good friend, Uncle Sam?"

"It's a joint partnership, we are sponsoring several doctors here, who wish to set up a mission. They are concerned about their safety, and the State Department is equally concerned, wo we are starting at the local level, with you. We are willing to pay for security which I understand you will provide, as well as a location for the clinic."

Mr. Sabi sat up even straighter, "You are well informed."

Kelly began the discussion about recent events. "One of the things State is the most concerned about are the recent tragedies that have occurred. We understand yesterday, a European businessman and his bodyguard were murdered on the road. We've been told, although we have no evidence, that it was a rogue militia group. It was our understanding that this gentleman frequented this area and had never had a problem before. So, I ask you quite directly, is this area safe?"

Kelly had a way of staring right into a man's eyes until she got some kind of an answer, which usually revealed something more than what they were ready to reveal. Sven had told Andy that she was the best interrogator he had ever met.

Mr. Sabi thought carefully, examining his fingers on the blotter in front of him. He began, "It depends on what kind of security is involved. We like to give our local police and fire extra work. In case we don't need them, they can still earn a decent living on the side working for other interests of our town. But as far as safety, if you run across a very well-armed militia group, these people who owe no loyalty to any particular country, it's very difficult, in fact sometimes nearly impossible."

"So, what you're saying is it's more expensive," answered Kelly bluntly without any emotion to her voice. "So how much would it cost to guarantee that a clinic would be able to operate without *any* kind of interference?"

"My dear, you do understand, that not all of the security money will go to the men who are actually doing the guarding. Some of it will need to be paid to certain groups who promise not to attack the clinic. As long as the money is paid, the clinic is safe."

"And this is guaranteed?" She asked.

"Guaranteed."

"And what sum are we thinking?"

"I would have to check with my superiors, but I believe something in the neighborhood of ten thousand dollars a day, might be able to be arranged? Do you suppose your uncle would be willing to pay for this service?"

"Yes, I think we are in the right ballpark. But I need to know who was responsible for the two kidnappings, first. The schoolgirls, I would like to know the location of the film crew that was taken seven days before. I need to know if they've been murdered, are being returned for ransom or if they're still alive, and I need to know if they're in this country or not. Based on your answers, we will agree to do business or not."

"This will take some time to gather all the information."

"We do not have a lot of time. We're ready to make a deal now. If, what you're saying, someone else has to make the decision, please direct me to that person."

Sabi stiffened, unused to being talked to in this manner, especially by an American, but a woman as well.

"I am that person. And you will have your answer tomorrow." His eyes narrowed.

Kelly turned around and left the office without asking anyone else's permission. Peterson, Andy and Sven followed her. Sven bowed to Mr. Sabi, "We'll be back tomorrow then?"

"I believe that will work. See you tomorrow, doctor." The Commissioner was fuming.

"No, it's Sven Tolar."

CHAPTER 23

JUST BEFORE SUNRISE, Aimee got the call she'd been hoping to get for days.

"You sound naked," Andy whispered.

"Oh God! Andy! I feel like it's been a year since we've talked."

"Only five days, but I'm losing track of things. Look, sweetheart, this has to be another quick call, but I'm good. Nothing to report. Just wanted to hear your voice."

"I have the very best news."

"Really?"

"We're rich, Andy. Carmen left me a boatload of money. Honey, we can travel, fix up the house, buy some investments. Andy, you can quit doing all that dangerous stuff. We can just be together, like we planned."

"But—"

"You'll never have to; I'll never have to work

again."

"Wait a minute. I didn't hear this right. You met with the attorney?"

"Yes, she passed day before yesterday. I visited with him yesterday morning and signed all the paperwork. I wasn't sure at first how I felt about it, but now that I've thought about what it could do for us, I see that it totally sets us free. You don't have to go on any of those dangerous missions anymore. I don't have to worry. I can get Logan into treatment again. It just opens up so many doors."

"But this is your money. She left it for you."

"That doesn't matter, Andy. It's our money."

"No, it's yours. It's not mine."

"I'm sharing it with you, so you don't have to do all that crazy stuff anymore."

"But I like what I do."

"Well, you could phase out, I mean, I wouldn't expect you to just quit. But you could."

Aimee heard nothing on the other end of the phone.

"Andy?"

"I don't want to quit."

"But you have to put your life on the line. It's dangerous, Andy. And you don't have to any longer."

"I don't do it to eat, or for us to live. I do it because I want to. Don't you understand? Haven't you learned anything about us?"

"I don't like your tone, Andy. You're making me scared."

"Aimee. You have to get a dose of reality here. What else am I good at? I've trained to do this. I want to do this for the next, well, I'm not due to re-up for a couple of years, but I want to stay with it. I like this job. And I don't particularly like the idea of being a kept man."

"Don't be silly. That's nonsense."

"It's not. You're already telling me what you want me to do. Do I ever pressure you?"

"No, but—"

"I don't like the feel of this. I'm going to have to think about this whole thing."

"What about us?"

"You're part of it. You're who I come home to, Aimee. I'm doing it for you, too."

"But wouldn't you rather be a man of leisure, spend all your time at the beach? Travel, see distant places, meet interesting people? Expand your knowledge of the world? Learn a bunch of languages, invest in our future? Doesn't any of that sound like what we talked about?"

She was getting nervous about the conversation and knew she had gone about this all wrong. Now that it was fully out, there was no taking it back. And the answer she got back confirmed it.

"That's exactly what I do now, Aimee. You've got to be kidding me. I mean, it's great having all that money, but I've seen interesting people, traveled the world. I like being a force for good. If you ask me would I enjoy just spending my time at the beach all day, or hanging out having cocktails and crab, I think I'd get bored."

"But we'd be together, Andy."

"But we're together now, sweetheart. I feel you here, right beside me. When I come home, it will be so great to be together again. We are a team now. And I want to be the support for the men I work with, men I care about. I don't think I could live with myself if I just sat around and did nothing just because I could. What kind of life is that?"

Her heart was racing, her blood pressure rising. She felt darkness in her chest, finding it hard to breathe. Black spots appeared in her eyes. She inhaled deeply and blew it out. Then did it again. That's when it hit her. Was he saying that his job was more important than their marriage?

"Unfortunately, I've got to go. And this sucks big time. I've probably said it all wrong, but I love you, Aimee. And if you love me, don't ask me to give up something I believe in doing. My work isn't done."

"I understand." She heard the whine in her voice

and hated herself for it.

"We need to talk about this, and I can't do it now. I'm sorry if I rained on your parade, but I've got to go."

He hung up without saying good-bye. She felt like she'd been hit across the face. How could he be so cold? Was this the reason she was hesitant to accept the money? Did she know something like this would happen?

Andy had never spoken to her this way before. And yes, he was right about a lot of things, but especially about her little special Happily Ever After bubble filled with unrealistic expectations. But she believed in things like magic, running in the direction of her dreams, making up stories and adventures and being inspired. Was it a mistake, then, to be partnered with a Man of Action, as he called himself? Could they have made a mistake getting together?

All throughout her run with Sandy it bothered her. The more steps she took, the more the hurt and anger festered. It wasn't fair, what he'd said. It was almost as if she'd done something bad. Why couldn't he celebrate what kind of freedom that money could bring to them? And did that mean—no—it couldn't be that! Did that mean that it would destroy them?

She hadn't considered the pride she heard in his voice. He didn't want to live off her money, that was clear as day.

Just as she entered the house, her phone rang.

"Aimee, I have some good news," Dr. Denby's voice should have been good news, but she resented his happy demeanor.

"Oh really? What?"

She cursed herself for being so lame. She was still knee deep and blood with the conversation with Andy that she wasn't present to him. This had to do with Logan.

"We've found him. He was picked up late last night. The sheriff called me, and we were able to pick him up this morning. I've got him on a mandatory lockdown for seventy-two hours. I can hold him longer if you'll sign off on it."

"So, he's at your center?"

"Yes. He's fighting a bit. I was thinking perhaps you should come over and see him. If you think it would do any good, I can try to find a permanent spot, get another scholarship for him and see what we can do for thirty days. After that, he's going to have to put in more of an effort. But I just wanted to call you and let you know he's safe, and we have another crack at getting him on the right track."

"Thank you, doctor. Maybe I should do that. My plans for today just blew up on me, so I'll be over in an hour. Will that work?"

"Perfect."

"So, how does this work? Will they allow you to keep him, or does he have to face charges?"

"I don't think they've filed anything. He's probably got one more chance. I'm not seeing his cooperation yet. Maybe you could convince him."

Well, she'd just perhaps blown up one relationship with the man she loved. She wasn't in the mood for this, but maybe it was exactly the right thing to do. She went to her bedroom and picked up the box of photographs her Realtor had sent over. Maybe some of these would be useful, she thought.

All the way over, she thought about her conversation with Andy. The wakeup call was bitter. The house and everything about the house was done with her own money, it was her idea, and he went along with it. But it wasn't what he would have done, and maybe she should have paid more attention to it. The comment about not wanting to be a kept man left her hollow inside. She'd never thought that she was doing that. Never once did it occur to her that he might be sensitive to the money she inherited. And now, she'd just exacerbated it like one hundred percent.

She gripped the steering wheel and tightened her jaw. Hearing Sandy move, she looked in the rearview mirror. That's when she got a good look at her face, streaked with lines and looking older, certainly not happy. It was the face like she'd seen on some of the wives—a face that scared her at first when she got introduced to the community. She'd been told it was hard, that loving a SEAL was not a casual thing. But for Aimee, it had never been like that.

But now she could see how complicated he was. And how completely caught unaware she was. What was she thinking?

The parking lot was full, so she had to drive around several times to find a spot. She grabbed Sandy's leash and prayed they'd let her take the dog into the hospital.

She'd been there the last time with Andy. She remembered that day. He'd been so caring, holding her hand, pressing her shoulders and letting her know he shared her pain over her brother's problems. It had been such a difficult day, and Andy had been right there for her.

Like she was supposed to be for him.

A male attendant dressed in white greeted her.

"Ma'am, I'm afraid we don't allow dogs here. As much as we love them, not everyone does, and we have to think about the guests and patients who come."

"I don't have any place I can keep her. I'm here just for a quick meeting with one of your patients. Could you call Dr. Denby first, and can we ask him?"

"Well, it's policy—Yes, Dr. Denby? You have someone in the lobby to see you." He put his hand over the phone. "Who should I say is here?"

"Aimee Carr."

"Oh, okay. Well, she has a dog with her, and we can't—"

He focused on the ceiling as he was given instructions.

"Very well." He hung up the phone. "He's coming right up to talk to you now."

"Thank you."

Dr. Denby came with a young technician wearing a lab coat. "Hey there, Aimee. This is one of my students, and she's agreed to watch the dog for a few minutes while you visit with Logan. Meghan, this is Aimee. And who's this?" He bent down and pet Sandy, who tried to give him her paw.

"Sandy. She's very well behaved and would love it."

As the two walked out the front doors, Dr. Denby escorted Aimee back into the clinic. He held a chart under his arm.

"He's having a medical evaluation now. We're taking blood, getting some clean clothes for him, checking for head lice, all standard stuff, sorry."

"No, I completely understand."

"We get kind of detailed here. That way we know what we're dealing with. It appears he might have lost considerable weight since we saw him last. Did you notice the same?"

"Yes."

"So, when you see him, don't react. We've also given him a haircut and he hates it."

"He probably hates being detained."

"Definitely. Now, I'm going to give you two a chance, but if he gets violent, I'm going to stop it, okay?"

"Absolutely. Do you think he's healthy otherwise?"

"I'm not ready to say that. Something's going on, but we'll have to wait for the tests." He turned the corner and stopped in front of a door marked Examination Room 6. "Ready?"

"Just a second. I've just learned I've come into some money, and I'll have the ability to have him stay here, if you think it will work. I'm willing to invest in him, but only once. How do we do that?"

"We can put him on rotating lockdowns, voluntary. The ones I've seen work best stay about six months. If they do the program that way, it usually sticks. But it's a lot of money, Aimee, I won't lie."

"Let's do it, but only if you think he'll accept it and work on it. Otherwise, it's a waste. Again, I can only do this one time, doctor. Only once."

"I got you. That's a very generous offer. I'll do my very best. So, are you ready?"

"As ready as I'll ever be." She was just about to put ten years searching for Logan behind her. She knew this was either an ending, or a beginning. She vowed to be okay with it either way.

As soon as the door opened, Aimee saw the shriveled, scruffy figure of her brother. Like the way he'd looked at the doorway last night, his eyes were sunken in, with dark grey circles beneath them. His cheeks sagged, and his eyes were partially glazed over. She thought the doctor might have given him something to calm him down but wasn't sure.

She sat across the table from him. "Logan? Do you remember me? I'm Aimee."

"I don't know you," he said.

"Yes, you do. You came by my house last night. And you made me this." She showed him the bracelet he'd left on her doorstep.

One hand came from under the table, his forefinger touching it, careful not to touch her skin.

"I wear it all the time and I think of you."

He pulled his hand back under the table and angled away from her. "You shouldn't. You should forget about me."

"It's not that easy, Logan. None of us every forgot you for one day. Every single day both mom and dad thought about you. They loved you so much. But you came back. You reached out, and now I'm here."

"Nobody can fix me."

"That's probably true, Logan. I know I can't. But I can love you. I know how to do that. I want to help you be able to feel it too, if it's possible."

He turned in his seat, scowling up at Dr. Denby, who was standing next to Aimee. "This your idea?"

"Sort of." He shrugged. "Logan, you're being held on a seventy-two-hour order. But I'm going to recommend you try a thirty day stay, and then decide if this is what you want or not. Because it has to be your decision. I'm not going to lie to you. I've been honest with Aimee when I told her that people who have done to themselves what you've done don't usually clean up on their own. Even our stats sort of suck."

"What's the point?"

"Well, to start with, there might be some underlying medical condition that's making your symptoms worse. I don't know. And we never got started because you walked away before the treatment was finished. I'm going to ask for more of a commitment from you this time."

"This must be your idea," he said to Aimee, sneering.

Aimee could feel her patience eluding her. It had been one ugly night, and this morning with the call with Andy making it worse, she didn't have the stomach for much more. She didn't hurt like she did before when she'd seen him. But she did care.

Maybe it was time to face reality.

"You know, Logan, you may not realize it, but you

were loved. And Mom and Dad tried to get you help, but it was too much. It cost them almost everything they had at the time, not that money is everything. But you reached out to me and I'd like to know why? What made you do this?" She held up the bracelet.

"I'm not sure. I like to walk the beach sometimes. I've seen you running there. I saw the wedding, that day. I stole some booze and grabbed a sandwich." He stopped, then finished with, "I wanted to do something human. Most days, I feel like an animal."

The cold icy crust covering her body melted. "Thank you, Logan. It is the most valuable piece of jewelry I own. I shall cherish it forever."

She let the tears run down her cheeks, let him see her and the hurt that was there. His eyes started to moisten, and then he looked away.

"If I never see you again, I just want to thank you also for this gift. For showing up again. For giving me the chance to tell you that I love you. I've gotten to know some people who never got that chance, some of them waiting for twenty years or more. Now, some might find that cruel. But I find it inspiring. Because they have hope, Logan. That's something I want to help you find again, because you were the most positive person I knew growing up. My big brother."

Dr. Denby inserted himself. "You're being offered a miracle, Logan."

"Some say life is a gift. Some say it's a curse."

"What do you think," Dr. Denby asked him.

"I've been on both sides of that argument." He looked down at Aimee's bracelet again. "I'd like to think of it as a gift, but I'm not sure I can handle it all the time. Sometimes people are just too damned happy. I hate that."

She saw the broken parts of his soul, the emptiness of his wandering.

"You're being given a chance. Do you want to take it?" the doctor asked.

"I don't like to make promises I can't keep."

"So, how's that going for you, Logan?" he asked again.

Logan shrugged, briefly checking Aimee's expression. "Sure, I like gifts. Miracles. Why not?"

"But you have to want to get better," Aimee said. "And maybe you can't. But I'm going to help you this one time, and then I'm done. You stay here until you get better and stronger. Not perfect. But you don't run away this time. You stay as long as you like, and I'll pay for it, Logan. But if you leave, I won't be there a second time. Those are my rules. But you have to agree to those rules."

At the end of their conversation, Logan consented to being voluntarily remanded to the clinic for four months, minimum, which Dr. Denby said could keep him out of jail, unless he escaped. He'd be locked in his room at night but given relative freedom in a secured location during the day. He'd submit to blood and urine testing and attend classes. They'd do a full medical diagnosis and try to adjust what they could. He was told it might not work, but if he wanted it to, there was no limit to what he could achieve.

Just before Aimee left, he called out to her.

"Will you come visit me?"

"I will, if you ask me to. I won't come unless you ask, Logan. But I'll come as much as I can, if you ask."

Aimee left the clinic, collecting Sandy on the way, and felt settled for the first time in months. She'd been lucky enough to play by her heart and have the chance to do something good with her money. Now the next battle was going to be settling with Andy. Having some honest conversations.

She still had hope. Of all people, today Logan gave her that hope.

CHAPTER 24

ANDY WAS SILENT on their way back to camp. Sven and Peterson were cracking jokes, off-color jokes, and Kelly was lowering the boom on them right and left. Sven seemed to enjoy getting her angry.

Andy wasn't in the mood.

"So, what's going on with you, Dr. Carr?" Sven asked.

"Oh, you know. Got five minutes to talk to my new bride, and we sort of have a fight. I think that's what it was."

"She'll get over it," Peterson said, slapping Andy's knee.

"No, I think I'm the one who has to get over it. I reacted to something she said, and damned if I'm being stubborn, but I think I was right."

Kelly turned around in the front seat. "Really? A man who thinks he's right. I've never heard that before. Why, don't you know, all men are right?"

She turned her back on the second seat, with the three Amigos sitting side by side. They'd just gotten their fanny slapped and nobody appreciated it.

"Maybe we better cool it for a bit. I think tensions are building, and we got to have all out wits about us tonight," offered Peterson. "But I'll tell you, that's happened to me a time or two. It takes a little adjustment sometimes for the wives."

"We've lived together for a year. I've been on one deployment before."

"Oh well, then, my gosh, a whole year? Why you should have everything figured out by now." Kelly was downright nasty tonight.

Andy was starting to hate her. He'd never liked women who were sporting attitude with him because there was no real sport in it. He wasn't allowed to really fight back. It was an old wound.

For the rest of the five minutes it took to return to base, no one said a word. Andy wondered what Adaze was thinking. He was a man still feeling the pain of losing his wife. It was like all of them were on different pages in different books in different libraries.

Peterson retreated to make his phone call. Andy sullenly ambled over to his cot.

"How'd it go?"

"Drama wasn't one of my better subjects in high school. I don't get this guy, Sabi. I'm standing there, listening to him cajole, and talk. I'm wondering to myself, what the hell are we doing here?"

"Whoa! Where'd that come from?"

"I'm a little short on patience today. I think I'm just probably tired. Mind if I catch some shuteye for a bit?"

"No, I'll leave you alone. You want some lunch?"

"Not really hungry. I'd rather sleep."

"Okay, I'll wake you if there's something else going on." Dallas left their room.

The other cot was for Sven, and Andy knew there was a fifty-percent chance he wouldn't be needing it tonight. It took mere seconds before he was in the pits of a deep, dark sleep.

WHEN ADAM AWOKE, Tucker was seated next to the cot with a plate of food.

"Come on, sport. You gotta eat something."

"I think I caught a bug."

"Yeah, that's what I heard. Well this stuff is damned tasty. You should try some. One of the Afri-corps wives makes it. Pretty good for you too. Try it."

Andy knew he was sulking. He accepted the plate and knew Tucker was sent when he started eating and the old guy didn't leave.

"I got in a huge argument with Brandy before I left. I'm going to have to fix that first thing when I get back."

"Pretty remarkable you volunteered for this, with a new baby in the house. I can only imagine. You'll probably get *all* the midnight feedings and diaper changes for a year, and even then, it won't be enough."

"Some guys during my first ten all re-upped at the same time so they could get their bonus and buy a fishing boat together. Not only did it not go over with the wives they forgot to consult, two of them actually got divorces and wound up having to spend the boat money for attorney's fees and child support."

"That's a cluster fuck if I've heard one." Andy finished his meal. "You wouldn't be trying to make me feel better, now would you?"

"Oh, it kinda crossed my mind. You've done a great job with these new buds, and they like you, Andy. I think you've made a real contribution. I'm gonna have to get even for the suggestion I come over to do this little TDI. But besides that, we're friends, and it warms my heart to see you've found a place here. You know how Kyle likes to keep things tight. I can see Peterson has a ways to go, but he's alright. He's learning. He listens, and that's the most important part. Nothing worse than someone being stupid and putting everyone's lives at risk."

"He's pretty good, I agree with you there."

"So, since Kyle's not your LPO yet, and I'm kind of senior here as far as years in, I thought, if you needed to, we could have a talk."

Andy didn't want to offend the big man, but he really didn't want to talk about the conversation he had with Aimee. But he decided to make a stab at it.

"Let me ask you this, Tucker. Did you ever find Brandy, when you guys were first getting together, like overly enthusiastic about really dumb shit?"

"You had an argument about *that?*"

Andy knew it was a feeble attempt. He shouldn't have tried, he knew better.

"Let me see, Brandy, yes, she can get worked up about stuff about the house, wanting to make it perfect. She went and had some plans drawn for a deck upstairs, the fencing for the rear yard, and heck, we didn't have more than two extra nickels at the end of the month. But damn it, somehow, she managed to get it done. Her dad was a big help. She found these three guys who love to build shit. They drew up the plans, got it through the city, and bingo, we had a beautiful deck, rear fencing, and a partial remodel. All I had to do was pay for materials. They do this pay-it-forward type of thing."

"So, she solves problems."

"No, I'd say she always looks for the opportunities. She sees the good in everyone. I used to see her try to be nice to those bitches who were her best friend's girlfriends. She never fit in. She's a big girl, as you know. Those ladies would dis her in ways she never figured out, but it didn't matter. She was always cool about it. Didn't whine and complain." Tucker erupted in a belly laugh.

"What is it?"

"Well, she likes to get even. She has fun with that. People are always underestimating her, too, and it doesn't matter. She's naturally happy. I have to have someone like that by my side. I don't like having to eke out my itty-bitty emotions and proper thinking for approval. She loves me. She always will. And man, the more we're together the more I love her right back."

Now Andy felt really bad. He'd been a total dick. It didn't matter if he was a poor SEAL or a rich SEAL. Being rich was going to be a whole lot better. Why the hell had he gotten so worked up?

"Thanks, man."

"For what? I didn't do anything."

Sven poked his head into the room. "We got a briefing starting now, Carr. We need all hands on."

THE INTEL RECEIVED during the last twenty-four hours confirmed that the film crew and the girls were being held at the abandoned school site. The whole team breathed a sigh of relief since the longer they were present in Benin, the more likely they'd run into someone who would want to pick a fight. But they had strength in numbers. Andy felt confident they had everything they needed.

Part of the team was to pack up and get ready to leave once they either did or did not get the hostages. Gunnar was not happy he was going to lose three trucks, but Kelly made sure he was properly compensated. Adaze was happy to be one of the drivers delivering them across the border, since he'd get another bonus. He offered to bring back one of the trucks along with a couple of corpsmen.

Peterson let Tucker and Sven set up the mission, and gave some good suggestions, based on what he'd been told of the school. Diku had once had a child who attended the school, so he gave them good information on the most likely areas to search first. What was most concerting was that there were at least twenty armed guards, and Peterson had been told more were on the way. It was do it tonight, or go away with nothing, possibly with injuries.

Tucker had Danny Begay and Armando positioned to pick off some of the guards with their long guns. Fredo was to blow up one of the guard huts where the drone had picked up the most bodies, but not in the heavy concentration like the other building, a former cafeteria, where they assumed the hostages were being held. It all had to be coordinated at the same split second. Then Tucker and his team would breach the building and start extracting hostages.

They were hoping everyone was healthy enough to walk. Diku, Adaze and another brother were to bring the vehicles closer, all loaded up, so they could bypass the UNESCO camp and just make a line for the border. If they had to, they could stop in Kandi for supplies or to treat the injured.

Danny and Armando found rooftops with perfect line of sight to the yard outside the hut and the hostage area. They divided up the guards they could see, using their Invisios. Fredo and Dallas set charges all over the place. They wired an ammunition storage locker that had been left open, all around the old office building housing the guards, and a diesel storage tank used for fuel. Archie located the generator and, on the mark, would cut the power, leaving most of the camp in pure darkness. With their NV goggles, the SEALs would have a huge advantage.

Sven gave the signal. In rapid succession, six shots, sounding like three, took out six outside guards, and then the two or three who ran outside afterwards. The charge was a little late and went off about a minute after the power was cut and the diesel tank exploded. But by that time, there was so much confusion that the element of surprise was no longer a factor.

Andy helped Tucker move out the girls, who were screaming and had to be calmed down. This was the part of the mission Andy wished they'd had the nurses. But as soon as the trucks arrived, they all climbed inside, helped by two of Diku's men. The five Dutch and American journalists were very weak and barely able to walk, but with help they were loaded into the two remainder trucks, and when all three vehicles left the camp, less than five minutes had gone by.

Not one guard at the school was left alive.

Peterson got word that a force was coming up from the South. It was decided that they bypass the UNESCO site, where they'd planned on dropping off the girls, and to head to Kandi and return them to the two nurses, who could treat them.

The Africacorp drivers were phenomenal, and Andy wanted to make sure when he got stateside that the Navy knew how well they worked. They dodged obstacles, occasionally a cow or goat in the road, avoided potholes, and kept a speed of nearly fifty miles an hour all through the bush, cutting across two grassy savannahs without the benefit of a road beneath them.

Armando and Danny were riding in the rear of the last truck to watch for followers or choppers, but luck was on their side and they made the rendezvous to the Kandi camp in record time.

All the guards had held, and several additional ones showed up. Kelly applied Uncle Sam's cash liberally, and when Sven hugged Flora and they all said good-bye to the schoolgirls, the whole place was erupting into a celebratory party. Diku said that word went out to several parents in Benot that their daughters were safe and were coming to pick them up.

Andy thanked the tall Africacorp leader, the one he wasn't sure he could trust.

"You come back, I be your driver again," he said in broken English.

"That's a promise, Diku. You did good. Uncle Sam thanks you. Stay out of trouble."

"Trouble? No, this is fun!" He laughed and ran to his crowd.

It took them another two hours to hit the Niger border. The border patrol was not out in full force, but there was a long line of lorries and commercial vehicles waiting to get through. The bottleneck was going to take an hour, which was way too long.

Kelly demanded they cut in line and when deposited at the barricaded gate, several truckers behind them started honking.

Sven turned to Andy. "Amazing what that woman can do with a badge and some cash. Just watch her work," he whispered.

Seconds later, guards were removing the big barriers and the two trucks were allowed to pass. At the Niger border, the State Department had already given them clearance and they were waved through without even stopping them.

Peterson turned to Adaze. "You make sure all these guys get back over the border together, or my ass will be on the line. We don't want any international incidents here."

Adaze grinned and gave Peterson the Peace sign. "No problem. We were on a special mission saving baboons for UNESCO!"

For some reason, everyone thought that was hilarious and nobody stopped laughing for nearly five minutes.

A cargo plane was waiting for them at the airstrip, the huge belly opening wide to accept the men, their equipment, and the hostages onto the plane. Andy watched through the tiny porthole as the big behemoth bellied up, took off, leaving the two white trucks and their African brothers in arms behind, waving.

It had been a week of very intense days, with little sleep and nothing in the way of luxuries. But Sven passed out some Norwegian chocolates to every member of the team.

"Don't believe what they tell you. The best chocolates in the world come from Norway."

CHAPTER 25

A IMEE DIDN'T GET a call from Andy. Instead, she got a call from Peterson's wife.

"Hey, Aimee. You and I have got to get together and talk. My husband just loves Andy, and what he's brought to this team."

"Thank you. I appreciate that."

"So, I'm calling to let you know they'll be flying in tomorrow at three PM, and to apologize that none of them had any time to call home. They've been in a big ol' bucket of bolts, and they'll probably arrive half deaf too. Andy is staying over in Norfolk, and then driving home Saturday."

"Okay, thanks."

"I'm sure he'll call you when he lands."

"Yes, I suppose so." But Aimee suspected that the reason Andy didn't call was for something entirely different.

"We just wanted you to know how much we appreciate you and Andy. And I'm going to have to make sure you get invited to some of our wives events. I've been remiss, and that's on me."

"Thank you. It's been pretty busy here, with the wedding and everything. We live so far away."

"Well, maybe you two should consider buying a house here in Little Creek. It's a wonderful community. Very military friendly, of course. That way, you could get involved in more of the Team things."

It was the last thing Aimee wanted to do. With the additional funds, perhaps purchasing something for him to stay in when he had to go up to trainings, or a place for her to go so she could be there when he returned made sense. But all those plans seemed so far away. She wasn't sure any of it would work out now. And she was exhausted. She just didn't want to make any more decisions until she had to.

She spent the rest of the day cleaning the house, changing the sheets on all three bedrooms upstairs, since Sandy usually liked to take her pick when Aimee was out shopping, and had slept on all of them. She didn't mind the dog hair and smell everywhere, but it wasn't what Andy would like. It could also be one more thing for him to get angry about.

Shelley stopped by, bringing some flowers.

"Okay, what did I do wrong?" Aimee asked, slightly wary.

"Nonsense, silly. Why, are you in a streak of pissing people off? I hardly believe that about you."

If you only knew.

"I just brought them because. You've had a pretty big week. And now that Andy will be coming home—"

"How did you know?"

"One of my friends at school has a son on Team 4 with Andy." She walked up to Aimee and took her by the shoulders. "Are you okay?"

She hated that Shelley had that radar that could detect when she was on inner shaky ground. Despite her self-admonition, she began to cry.

"Oh, honey. I didn't mean to upset you, sweetheart."

Shelley was a good friend, but a lousy hugger. Her skinny frame was just too bony and fragile. There was only one person in Aimee's world who could hug a woman like she should be hugged.

Shelley put the flowers down, took Aimee by the hand and sat her down on the yellow couch so they could watch the bay together. "Tell me. I promise to only listen this time. I know I've been a pain and a half, and my advice has been shoved down your throat. You tell me. What's wrong?"

"I had a difficult call with early this morning. And then, I went down to Sarasota to visit Logan, and—"

"They found him?"

"Yes, he's in the treatment program there. He looks bad, Shelley. I just hope they can help him. But at least the money I get will be good for something."

"What did you say?"

"I meant, I can afford to help him out now. I couldn't have before."

Shelley stared out at the waves. "I shouldn't ask this, but is everything with you and Andy okay?"

"I think so. This was a hard trip. He was under lots of pressure."

"But certainly, you told him the good news?"

Aimee disentangled her fingers from Shelley's lap and smiled. "I did, and I was surprised with his reaction."

"I shouldn't pry."

"He doesn't want to be a 'kept man' as he put it. I thought he'd like to get off the Teams, retire. We could travel, do things around here, see the world a bit. Buy some property and fix it up."

"But. There's a but in there somewhere."

"There is. He likes his job."

"Nothing wrong with that."

"I think it's more important than me. I just realized that."

"No, here I think you're wrong. I've seen the way he looks at you. He's completely nuts about you. You know, telephone calls can be strange, especially when they only have a couple of minutes to catch up. You probably just had a bad connection, that's all."

"Yes. It was a bad connection. I misunderstood him. So, it won't be the happy homecoming like I expected. Instead, we have to talk some things out. I think we will."

"But you're worried about it."

"Think about it, Shelley. We live twelve hours away from his job. Who does that?"

"Airline pilots. Senators, Congressmen. Lots of people do. Professional athletes live clear across country sometimes."

"But it's a community. And it's important to him. For the first time I feel like my pull here, to this house, might be coming between us. I don't think it means the same for him."

"It never does. A house is way more important to a woman than a man. A woman has to feel like she has a place of her own. I've read lots of books on that. Trust me, I know."

Aimee smiled at her friend. She would have said that they were identical personality types, but now she saw that Shelley was also just as upbeat and positive, but far more realistic. It was hard to convey exactly what she was feeling. Maybe Shelley would never understand.

"It's more than the house. It's the disconnection to

the community. That's the problem and I didn't realize it until I spoke to him."

"Do you think you'd move up there?"

"No. I won't sell this house. This place is too special for me. He moved to Team 4 to be closer to here, but now I'm afraid, it might still be too far. But we'll see. I just need to make sure it's what he wants to do, and I'd just been assuming before."

"And now with Logan in Sarasota, there's another reason you might want to stay here."

"And we both know how that could turn out, too." Aimee leaned back on the couch, closing her eyes. "Argh. It's so complicated all of a sudden."

"Well, you have more choices now. Maybe one of them will work out. If not, I happen to know of a very deserving teacher who would love to inherit a small fortune." She followed it up with a smirk.

That did make Aimee laugh. "All right. Lecture's over. And I don't want to talk about anything sad. Bring me some good news."

"Oh, I forgot. I've got a new boyfriend. He's a single dad of one of my students. He's gorgeous, Aimee. You'd like him."

"We'll look forward to meeting him. You'll have to bring him by."

"I will once I feel I'm more secure. One look at you, and he might jump ship."

"Not a chance, Shelley. Come on, you were always the one they liked better."

"And you're a horrible liar."

SHE TOOK SANDY out for a run. On the way back, she passed a new used bookstore that had just opened up on Gulf Boulevard. In the window was an old, blue IBM Selectric typewriter, surrounded by Hank Borges books, with a black and white picture of Hank sitting at the table, using that typewriter to write one of his novels. It was taken from his backside, so it showed the view from the living room of the house she owned. The beach in the background was identical to the beach she saw every day.

She left Sandy tied to a bike rack outside where she could see her from inside the store. A clerk came up to her.

"May I help you find something?"

"I was looking at that display in the window. The typewriter, and Hank Borges books."

"Yes. That's the very typewriter he wrote those books on. Right here, in Sunset Beach."

"Did you know him?"

"No, he was way before my time. My mother met him a time or two. He was well liked."

"Did you ever see him with a woman?"

"No. I think he had a wife and children up north

somewhere. I've never seen a picture of him with a woman before."

"How did you get the typewriter?"

"It belongs to the owner here. I think it was given to him when Hank died. It's for sale, if you're a fan."

"For sale?"

"Yes. Everything in this store is for sale. Even the store. The owner is moving back to be closer to family in New Jersey. He's ready to retire."

"How much for the typewriter?"

"He's asking forty bucks."

"Sold. Can I come by later and pick it up with the car?"

"Absolutely. Oh, Mr. Nichols will be delighted it went to a fan."

"Tell him, I might be interested in the store, too. But I have to talk to my husband first."

"That would be the best piece of news he's had all year. Can I take your number so he can call you?"

Aimee wrote her address and phone number down for the owner. "I promise to be back before dark."

THE NEXT MORNING, Aimee came downstairs with Sandy, ready for another run. She liked the look of the blue typewriter placed in the middle of her dining room table. Next to it on the right, she had a stack of fresh white paper. To the left, she had a box ready to accept completed pages of a novel she had yet to write.

During her run, she passed by the bookstore, all of the surf shops not yet open, a diner serving breakfast and several real estate offices in a row. Landscapers were leaf blowing sidewalks. The free bus from St. Pete to Clearwater passed by, nearly empty. The pulse of the beach community was beginning to increase, with more and more snowbirds coming back to this special place every day. Signs began to pop up in the windows reading, "Snowbirds Welcome" or "Snowbirds Specials" to attract the new inhabitants.

She was guarding herself, waiting to learn when he'd return. She asked herself whether she could give up all this, if he insisted she come live with him in Little Creek. She would want to say yes. But part of her knew that if he made her give up something she loved so much that it wouldn't last anyhow.

And then she understood how Andy felt about his Team of brothers.

CHAPTER 26

T HE TWELVE-HOUR DRIVE from Norfolk to the Gulf Coast in Florida would give Andy lots of time to think, and he toyed with the idea of just coming home, unannounced. But that wouldn't be fair to her, to either of them.

He'd tried to sleep all the way home, but the hot and sticky ride in that transport wasn't ever comfortable, even with headphones, a dozen pillows and blankets. At least the Navy equipped it with blankets.

He took a shower in the team building and headed out to the parking lot.

Aimee picked up on the first ring. "Hello?"

His heart melted the instant he heard her, just like the first time they'd met, when she belonged to someone else, when she wasn't his to take. Every fiber of his being screamed out that she was the one, and how he knew that he would never be able to tell. But his body and soul knew. It had never wavered in that.

Just hearing her voice again seemed to bridge that gap, like the bridge that led to St. Pete and the Gulf communities beyond.

"I'm headed home. I'd ask to stop and pick up something from the store, but it would melt or go bad by the time I made it, but I'll ask again. Do you want anything on the way home?"

"Just you, Andy. You are the only thing I want in this whole wide world."

It was what he expected and didn't have any right to have. He never wanted to possess her, clip her wings or make her do anything she didn't want to do. He liked that she was easily inspired. He wanted more than anything to be that inspiration.

But first they had to have that talk.

"Can't wait, sweetheart. I'll be driving all night, see you in the morning. So, sleep naked."

After they hung up, he smiled. She was easy to please, easy to love. His life would forever be a better one if she was by his side. And it would only work if she was happy too. So that's what they would talk about, explore together.

He listened to jazz all the way home. And, before the sun was even warming a tiny part of the ocean at the horizon, he pulled onto Gulf Boulevard, which was completely devoid of traffic. He let the magic pull him back to the house on Sunset Beach.

He opened the living room door and was instantly greeted by a big yellow dog who barked at him.

"So much for a stealth entrance. Hello. What's your name?"

The big dog handed him her paw. Andy got on his knees and felt the fluffy fur around her ears and neck.

"That's Sandy," Aimee said from the top of the stairs.

He dropped his duty bag and ran up the stairs to greet her properly. Sandy followed right along, step by step. He took her face in his hands, and pressed against her lips, the luxuriated in the loving feel of her soft, body. He'd forgotten how good she smelled, what her hair felt like when he laced his fingers through it.

She was crying.

"What's wrong?"

"I'm just so happy to see you. I thought—"

"Don't ever believe anything I tell you when I'm about to do battle," he whispered. "It's all bullshit."

"But—"

He cut her off with another kiss. "I'm sorry, Aimee. I was a complete asshole. This one was my fault."

"But—"

"It's all good. I need to sleep with the woman I love. You're my prize, my reason for coming home, sweetheart. Will you accept me, imperfect as I am?"

"Oh, Andy, always. I've never wavered. I'm sorry, if

I upset you."

"You know that saying on your wall? *The ocean heals everything.* That's the truth, Aimee. And you're right, this house is magic. You make it my magic."

She stripped off her nightie while he undressed, and then slipped under the covers to lay on top of her, allowing her flesh and soft places to wear off all the rough parts of the past few days. He kissed her neck. He kissed that fragrant place between her breasts where she wore her perfume. She arched, bent her knees and tilted her pelvis to accept him.

And Sandy hopped on the bed right next to them.

"So, this is going to be a threesome from now on?"

Aimee was laughing so hard, Andy thought perhaps he'd lost his opportunity to have a little romance.

"She sleeps on the bed, too? Dog hair and everything?" he asked her.

"Yes. But we could convert the other bedroom into her room, if you like."

Andy got up, thought about it for a minute and then answered, "Yes, I like." He called to the dog, walked her to the bedroom next door and closed the door.

While the dog whined and barked until sunrise, Andy and Aimee rekindled the flame that had never really gone out. Wherever she wanted to live, he told her, is where they would live.

When they made love for the second time, she brought up the subject of buying him a little house in Virginia. "Some place for when you have to be there, some place where I can come visit and surprise you. As long as you come home to me."

"You'd do that for me?" he said as his rhythm increased.

"I'd do anything for you. I'd be your kept woman."

"Except you'd be paying for the house."

"I'd let you pay for the whipped cream and pancakes in the morning. That's only fair, Andy."

"Oh, pancakes, and syrup, all over your body. Hardly seems a fair trade."

"I negotiate well."

"I love the way you negotiate."

"So, this will still be our home?"

"Of course. Always."

As long as she was okay with him staying on the teams, he'd drive that twelve-hour drive home after every mission if he had to, with or without a house in Virginia.

"Because, Aimee, I want to be part of your life when you're the happiest. And you're the happiest here, at Sunset Beach."

Did you love The House at Sunset Beach?

Stay tuned for the audio book,
which will be coming soon.

And stay tuned to the rest of the Sunset SEALs series,
as all four couples get to tell their stories,

About Sunset Beach.
authorsharonhamilton.com/sunset-seals

If you want to start in the beginning of this series, read
Book 1, SEALed At Sunset, where Andy and Aimee's
story begins.

ABOUT THE AUTHOR

 NYT and USA Today best-selling author Sharon Hamilton's award-winning Navy SEAL Brotherhood series have been a fan favorite from the day the first one was released. They've earned her the coveted Amazon author ranking of #1 in Romantic Suspense, Military Romance and Contemporary Romance categories, as well as in Gothic Romance for her Vampires of Tuscany and Guardian Angels. Her characters follow a sometimes rocky road to redemption through passion and true love.

Now that he's out of the Navy, Sharon can share with her readers that her son spent a decade as a Navy SEAL, and he's the inspiration for her books.

Her Golden Vampires of Tuscany are not like any vamps you've read about before, since they don't go to ground and can walk around in the full light of the sun.

Her Guardian Angels struggle with the human charges they are sent to save, often escaping their vanilla world of Heaven for the brief human one. You won't find any of these beings in any Sunday school class.

She lives in Sonoma County, California with her husband and her Doberman, Tucker. A lifelong organic gardener, when she's not writing, she's getting *verra verra* dirty in the mud, or wandering Farmers Markets looking for new Heirloom varieties of vegetables and flowers. She and her husband plan to cure their wanderlust (or make it worse) by traveling in their Diesel Class A Pusher, Romance Rider. Starting with this book, all her writing will be done on the road.

She loves hearing from her fans:
Sharonhamilton2001@gmail.com

Her website is:
sharonhamiltonauthor.com

Find out more about Sharon, her upcoming releases, appearances and news when you sign up for Sharon's newsletter.

Facebook:
facebook.com/SharonHamiltonAuthor

Twitter:
twitter.com/sharonlhamilton

Pinterest:
pinterest.com/AuthorSharonH

Amazon:
amazon.com/Sharon-Hamilton/e/B004FQQMAC

BookBub:
bookbub.com/authors/sharon-hamilton

Youtube:
youtube.com/channel/UCDInkxXFpXp_4Vnq08ZxMBQ

Soundcloud:
soundcloud.com/sharon-hamilton-1

Sharon Hamilton's Rockin' Romance Readers:
facebook.com/groups/sealteamromance

Sharon Hamilton's Goodreads Group:
goodreads.com/group/show/199125-sharon-hamilton-readers-group

Visit Sharon's Online Store:
sharon-hamilton-author.myshopify.com

Join Sharon's Review Teams:

eBook Reviews:
sharonhamiltonassistant@gmail.com

Audio Reviews:
sharonhamiltonassistant@gmail.com

Life is one fool thing after another.
Love is two fool things after each other.

REVIEWS

romantic, entertaining and very satisfying to read. It had me anticipating what would happen next many times over, so much so I could not put it down and even finished it up in a day. The vampires in this book were different from your average vampire, but I enjoy different variations and changes to the same old stuff. It made for a more unpredictable read and more adventurous to explore! Vampire lovers, any paranormal readers and even those who love the romance genre will enjoy Honeymoon Bite."

"This is the first non-Seal book of this author's I have read and I loved it. There is a cast-like hierarchy in this vampire community with humans at the very bottom and Golden vampires at the top. Lionel is a dark vampire who are servants of the Goldens. Phoebe is a Golden who has not decided if she will remain human or accept the turning to become a vampire. Either way she and Lionel can never be together since it is forbidden.

I enjoyed this story and I am looking forward to the next installment."

"A hauntingly romantic read. Old love lost and new love found. Family, heart, intrigue and vampires. Grabbed my attention and couldn't put down. Would definitely recommend."

PRAISE FOR THE
SEAL BROTHERHOOD SERIES

"Fans of Navy SEAL romance, I found a new author to feed your addiction. Finely written and loaded delicious with moments, Sharon Hamilton's storytelling satisfies like a thick bar of chocolate." —Marliss Melton, bestselling author of the *Team Twelve* Navy SEALs series

"Sharon Hamilton does an EXCELLENT job of fitting all the characters into a brotherhood of SEALS that may not be real but sure makes you feel that you have entered the circle and security of their world. The stories intertwine with each book before...and each book after and THAT is what makes Sharon Hamilton's SEAL Brotherhood Series so very interesting. You won't want to put down ANY of her books and they will keep you reading into the night when you should be sleeping. Start with this book...and you will not want to stop until you've read the whole series and then...you will be waiting for Sharon to write the next one." (5 Star Review)

"Kyle and Christy explode all over the pages in this first book, *[Accidental SEAL]*, in a whole new series of SEALs. If the twist and turns don't get your heart jumping, then maybe the suspense will. This is a must read for those that are looking for love and adventure with a little sloppy love thrown in for good measure." (5 Star Review)

PRAISE FOR THE
BAD BOYS OF SEAL TEAM 3 SERIES

"I love reading this series! Once you start these books, you can hardly put them down. The mix of romance and suspense keeps you turning the pages one right after another! Can't wait until the next book!" (5 Star Review)

"I love all of Sharon's Seal books, but *[SEAL's Code]* may just be her best to date. Danny and Luci's journey is filled with a wonderful insight into the Native American life. It is a love story that will fill you with warmth and contentment. You will enjoy Danny's journey to become a SEAL and his reasons for it. Good job Sharon!" (5 Star Review)

PRAISE FOR THE
BAND OF BACHELORS SERIES

"*[Lucas]* was the first book in the Band of Bachelors series and it was a phenomenal start. I loved how we got to see the other SEALs we all love and we got a look at Lucas and Marcy. They had an instant attraction, and their love was very intense. This book had it all, suspense, steamy romance, humor, everything you want in a riveting, outstanding read. I can't wait to read the next book in this series." (5 Star Review)

"Dear FATHER IN HEAVEN,

If I may respectfully say so sometimes you are a strange God. Though you love all mankind,

It seems you have special predilections too.

You seem to love those men who can stand up alone who face impossible odds, Who challenge every bully and every tyrant ~

Those men who know the heat and loneliness of Calvary. Possibly you cherish men of this stamp because you recognize the mark of your only son in them.

Since this unique group of men known as the SEALs know Calvary and suffering, teach them now the mystery of the resurrection ~ that they are indestructible, that they will live forever because of their deep faith in you.

And when they do come to heaven, may I respectfully warn you, Dear Father, they also know how to celebrate. So please be ready for them when they insert under your pearly gates.

Bless them, their devoted Families and their Country on this glorious occasion.

We ask this through the merits of your Son, Christ Jesus the Lord, Amen."

By Reverend E.J. McMalhon S.J. LCDR, CHC, USN
Awards Ceremony SEAL Team One
1975 At NAB, Coronado

Made in the USA
Monee, IL
29 December 2020

55910419R00174